Also by Richard Katzev

Promoting Energy Conservation
Anecdote and Evidence
In the Country of Books
A Sense of Place
A Literary Collage
A Commonplace Book Primer
Other Lives, Other Times
The Observer
The Pleasures of Reading
The Preoccupations
Just to Be There: Summers in Italy

Essays on Literature

Richard Katzev

Table of Contents

The Reader 1

Marks in the Margin 13

Journey Through the Book 25

Annotating Ian McEwan's Saturday 39

Waiting for the New Yorker 57

My Fiction Friends 71

An Inquiring Mind 85

On Literary Truth 97

Philosophical Novels 107

Does Literature Change Lives? 123

The truth of fictional characters moves us because it is our own truth. Furthermore, great works of literature teach us about ourselves because they are scorchingly honest, as honest as any clinical data: the great novelist ... is ultimately highly self-revelatory. Thornton Wilder once wrote: If Queen Elizabeth or Frederick the Great or Ernest Hemingway were to read their biographies, they would exclaim, Ah—my secret is still safe. But if Natasha Rostov were to read War and Peace she would cry out, as she covered her face with her hands, How did he know? How did he know?

Irvin Yalom

Preface

In most critical discussions of literature, the experience of the reader is virtually ignored since literary scholars tend to dwell on the meaning of the text from various theoretical or cultural frameworks. Instead, in this collection of essays on literature, I focus on the experiences I have had in reading literature, how it has entered my life, and affected me.

At the outset it is important to understand why I read. In describing why she liked reading the novels of the French writer Colette, Vivian Gornick said: *"It was the potential for self-recognition that made Collette's novels so compelling."*

Of course, there are many other ways to answer that question. Each of us has our own reasons. What are mine? Why have I always been a reader, indeed, more so now than ever?

In *Night Train to Lisbon,* Gregorious asks: *"Was it possible that the best way to make sure of yourself was to know and understand someone else?"*

By his action, he answers affirmatively. And so he abruptly leaves his teaching position in Switzerland and heads off to Lisbon in order to learn as much as he can about the life of Amadeu Prado, the author of *A Goldsmith of Words,* the book he found through a remarkable set of circumstances in a Bern bookshop

As I think back upon all the literary reading I tried to do while I was teaching, I also have to answer affirmatively to Gregorious' question. I realize now that I was reading literature to better understand myself, something I rarely found in the discipline of psychology that I studied for so many years.

Rather, I discovered myself in the novels and stories I read. And as my reading continued, that awareness became clearer and I realized this was the place I had been seeking for quite some time. I believe it was a true discovery and not simply a creation.

In an interview on CBC, Tim Parks is reported to have said:

> *The reason why we like a book is because we say, Yes, because life is like that, and the reason why we stop reading certain kinds of childish books is because we say, Good story but life's not like that. The whole question of recognition is terribly important and that's why as you get older your reading experience inevitably gets richer because you have more of your own experience to bring to it.*

As I grow older, that is exactly what I am finding to be the case, especially now that I find myself recapturing memories that for so long had remained hidden. The continuing sense of recognition, some new, some old, is one of the reasons I continue to find the experience of reading literature so compelling.

The following ten essays illustrate the way literature has given me that sense of personal recognition that others have written about. They were written over the course of six years, with the first in 2009 and one other this year. I present them in the hope they will lead other readers to find their own sense of recognition in the experience of reading literature.

The Reader

"I live with books more than with people. Which is to say that I can easily do without people (there are days when I could easily do without myself), and that in the country of books where I dwell, the dead can count entirely as much as the living."

Adrienne Monnier

Once I left the academic community, I began reading literary fiction in earnest. In the early morning when it is still dark, I resume reading whatever novel or short story I had put down the night before. I get back to it if I am lucky enough to have an afternoon nap and then once again at night before I fall asleep. I also read serious non-fiction literature, especially the literature, if you can call it that, of the social sciences, such as the books and journal articles that deal with the research I am doing

But it is literary fiction that occupies the major portion of my reading time now. On average, I estimate that I spend about two and a half hours a day reading fiction. It is difficult to know how that compares with other readers. The recent National Endowment of the Arts report[1] on literary reading in this country is silent about the *time* spent reading. Instead, variations in the book reading habits of the adults sampled were

---

[1] Reading at Risk: A Survey of Literary Reading in America. National Endowment of the Arts. Research Division Report #46. 2004

measured in terms of *frequency* of books (literary and non-literary) read per year.

Four categories of readers were distinguished on the basis of books read per/year: light readers (1-5), moderate readers (6-11), frequent readers (12-49), and avid readers (50 or more). On that measure, I would most likely be considered a frequent reader. I am also a slow reader. In 2003, the year after the one reported in NEA Survey, I read 45 books, not quite enough to be considered an avid reader, at least in terms of completed *books*, not total time spent reading.[2]

With all the reading I've been doing lately, I have been led to wonder how and to what extent this kind of experience has influenced my life. How have my beliefs or values been changed by books I have read? Do I behave any differently than I would had I not been a reader of literary fiction? And why does literary fiction have such a powerful hold on me?

It is said that questions like these impossible to answer, that the effects of literature are too subtle to be measured and difficult to isolate from many other factors that shape a person's life. Perhaps. But more likely, I think we haven't really looked at these questions as carefully as we might. The difficulty of capturing the effects of reading literature doesn't mean it can't be done. Rather it suggests that we need to explore the issue with greater ingenuity than we have in the past and consider other ways to

---

[2] A complete measure would take into account time spent reading periodicals, newspapers, and material on the Web which taken together would be fairly substantial in my case.

examine the effects of the reading experience other than comparing groups of readers and non-readers.

I have come to believe that the major barrier to a clearer understanding of this issue is one of measurement, namely, how to identify the complex and subtle ways reading literature influences particular individuals. Following a long tradition of "self-study" in psychology and psychoanalysis, I am going to start this inquiry by looking as closely as I can at my own reading experience. How has reading literature affected me and to what extent has it made a difference in my life?

It is said that the right book at the right time can give rise to a lifelong reading habit. I have always wondered if Alexander Dumas' *Camille* was that book for me. I think I was about 14 or 15 when I read the novel. As I recall the situation, the 1937 movie with Greta Garbo as Camille had been reissued and for reasons that completely baffle me now, I decided that I wanted to see it. I am fairly certain my mother suggested I should read the book first and that she had purchased a copy for me.

And so, after breakfast early one weekend morning, I went back to bed to begin reading the novel. Going back to bed after breakfast was not something I ever did. That day was *the* exception and other than when I have been ill, I've never done it again. Reading *Camille* during the day in bed seemed like such a lark. Everything seemed to fall into place on what was no doubt a sunny Saturday in Los Angeles sometime during the early fifties.

I returned to the book after lunch and continued reading until I had finished by mid-afternoon, in plenty of time to see the film that evening. It was showing at a nearby art house and I know that I went alone. Now, more than fifty years later, tales of ill-fated romances and their screen adaptations continue to be among my favorites. What draws me to these literary works, as well as many so other forms of literary fiction?

There are times like that when a book nearly takes command of my life, when my day is measured only by the time remaining before I can get back to it. There is nothing remarkable about this; every dedicated reader feels the same. It is why reading is such an imperative, one that continues to delight and please throughout each year. Not long ago I went out of town for a few days to work on a project that was as remotely associated with literature as Newtonian physics. I was halfway through Azar Nafisi's *Reading Lolita in Tehran* and couldn't wait to get back to it.

The book brought alive the meaning of literature for those who could only read and discuss it in hiding. Within an hour after returning, I took up the book once again. A feeling of relief swept over me, an emotion I often feel in getting back to fiction. I am not sure what gives rise to this feeling. But I know it is never one I experience in reading books about social research, even an excellent one. Perhaps it is unfair to expect they would have that kind of effect. All I know is that when I am reading works of literary fiction I have this sense of being in a place that is both comforting and congenial.

In the beginning of my adult reading years, I know it was literature's other-worldliness that drew me to it. It was a world so very different than the world of perception, learning, and social influence that occupied my working day. The writing was fresh and often brilliant. It was alive. Literature puts me in a frame of mind and mood that I don't want to leave, and where I feel I belong. The colors are brighter, the rhythms are more surprising, the dialogue is richer. It is better than life itself.

The people are also so much more amusing and thoughtful than those I usually encounter. It never seems to matter that they live on the page. In fact, I soon come to realize I prefer it that way. Who would want to trade knowing a demolitions expert fighting the fascists in the mountains of Spain for a classical conditioning theorist in the basement of the Psychology Building?

In these books I find individuals who I never seem to come across in my ordinary life, people who I would like to know and talk to with a while. It is a treat to know them. They are always there, reading to take up where we last left them, full of sparkling with and thoughtful commentary. They don't shut of insult me with a nasty work or sly innuendo. And from time t time they say something that surprises me, set be back for a moment of reflection or confirms some belief I have. This is very reassuring. At least I haven't gone off the deep end entirely.

But there is also another reason I'd rather be reading literature, one that in the final analysis is far more important. Literature seems to get me closer to the truth of things, to the truth about other people and above all to the truth about myself more than anything else I encounter. In a way, literature has given me some degree of clarity about who I am and the several selves I have become. The discovery of these truths is the heart of my reading experience and I wouldn't continue reading literature if I didn't come across one every once in a while.

To be sure, I never know when I will chance upon such a truth or in what books they will appear. Their discovery is unpredictable, unexpected, compelling.

Recently, I spent some time trying to figure out what leads me to these truths. In doing so, I thought I would gain some understanding of the concept of literary truth, as well as the reasons why I have succumbed to the literary experience. Of course, some of these truths are simply written so beautifully that they are hard to ignore, while others may be so witty or funny that I wanted to make note of them. But the majority convey an important truth that I wanted to record in order to mull over again at some later date.

I have no doubt that I have learned a very great deal from the books I have read. That includes a good deal of factual information, knowledge of other individuals and groups, styles of living and once again, a better understanding of myself. But I don't read literature to learn in the same way I read a chemistry textbook to master the periodic table. Rather what I have learned is a rather disorganized store of information acquired as a result of an informal learning process, rather than anything quite deliberate.

I also think that what I have learned from literature has varied as a function of my age. I didn't know anything about hypocrisy or the ubiquity of "phoniness" when I read *The Catcher in the Rye* as an adolescent. Afterwards I saw it everywhere. I still do. And I knew nothing about alienation or the sense of absurd until I read *The Stranger* not long after. While these concepts and others like them do not dominate my thinking, they do remain quietly in the background in my view of things.

In reading fiction I spend a fair amount of time considering the matters it sets before me. I suppose that literature is no different in this respect than any other learning experience. But somehow it seems more intimate, more personal, more likely to encourage an interior dialogue on some idea. The experience is not unlike the one Jonathan Franzen described in reading Alice Munro:

> *"Reading Munro puts me in that state of quiet reflection in which I think about my own life: about the decisions I've made, the things I've done and haven't done, the kind of person I am, the prospect of death."*

The more often this occurs, the more I like the book. Sometimes these musings clarify uncertainties I have or suggest other ways to view the matter. At other times, they simply confirm beliefs I hold. It is always good to know they make some sense and that others share them, even if they live in another world.

I have also learned from my recent introduction to literature how little of it I know and how much catching up I have to do. I try to read across a broader range than I did 25 years ago. Then it was largely the *New Yorker*, if I was lucky. Now it extends to modern novels, and short stories, some poetry, a few theatrical productions, the classics--a little Tolstoy, Chekhov, and Proust--and the moderns--Coetzee, McEwan and Roth.

When I find an author whose work I like, I am likely to begin collecting his or her other works. A favorable review and the author's books are in my "cart;" an enticing ad and the collection grows, reference to a "must read" or an "influential forerunner" still more is added to the order, until eventually it is time to ship it out.

Reading good literature has also encouraged me to write, at least to try. I read terrific pieces of writing and I wonder if I could write like that? Of course I can't, but reading those who do it ever so much better makes it seem all the more worthwhile. And so I try this, I try that, I make errors, I get a little better. There is nothing like the experience. The act of reading literature encourages me to keep trying. Surely that is one of its strongest influences upon me.

The emotional and intellectual sensibilities that I have acquired from my reading experiences are difficult to identify with any degree of certainty. Here again I may be wrong to assume such effects, but it is hard not to attribute them to the cumulative impact of reading experiences. The problem is how to describe such an elusive notion as sensibility in a way it can be measured or clearly communicated and to isolate the influence of literature from the several other factors that surely play a role.

You can see examples in individuals who have a way with words and are extremely well read. In my view, Susan Sontag was one such person. So is Harold Bloom. And it is clearly absent in other individuals who display none of their literary sophistication. But what is it that they have that I don't? They have surely read more widely, written about it more extensively, talked to students and literary scholars far more than I. They have spent a lifetime doing these things and above all they are quite simply just smarter than I am.

Although many people claim they have read a book that has changed their life, I can't think of a single one that has had such an effect on me. I do know reading a collection of great books in my Freshman Western Civilization course did fix the direction of my life. After that, there was no turning back from the life of learning and research. This is a path that I have taken at the expense of many others. Each step along that path strengthened their effects. The cumulative impact of those experiences, week after week, year after year must be enormous. It is especially so in comparison to the experiences I might have had if I had not been reading. Instead, I read, ponder, take notes, do some research, and ruminate.

So rather than directly shape specific beliefs or values that I may hold, I think literature has exerted its influence in a much more general way. For example, my notions of love, justice, morality and beauty are hard to pin down. They tend to be much more fluid and tend to shift around a bit depending my experiences and the situation in which I find myself. The readings I have done have also taught be to be more critical, to become more receptive of different ideas, cultures and ways of being.

It is in these various ways that I have been drawn to literature. I see people who are much like I am. Their companionship is revealing and consoling both. I see them more clearly than those I encounter in my daily life who I see only on the surface. There is something about a work of fiction that reveals the truth of a person as well, if not better, than any other account. Janet Malcolm in her beautiful volume *Reading Chekhov: A Critical Journey* put this well:

> "We never see people in life as clearly as we see the people in novels, stories, and plays; there is a veil between ourselves and even our closest intimates, blurring us to each other. But intimacy we mean something much more modest than the glaring exposure to which the souls of fictional characters are regularly held up. We know things about Gurov and Anna—especially about Gurov, since the story is told from his point of view—that they don't know about each other, and feel no discomfort in our voyeurism. We consider it our due as readers. It does not occur to us that the privacy rights we are so nervously anxious to safeguard for ourselves should be extended to fictional characters."

In her recent book, *Leave Me Alone, I'm Reading*, Maureen Corrigan writes that we read "...to set off on a search for authenticity. We want to get closer to the heart of things and sometimes even a few good sentences...can crystallize value feelings, fleeting *physical sensations, or sometimes, profound epiphanies."*

Harold Bloom in *How to Read and Why* concurs. *"Ultimately we read—as Bacon, Johnson, and Emerson agree—in order to strengthen the self, and to learn its authentic interests."* Yes, we don't have an easy time knowing ourselves. Sometimes a good book makes our task a little easier, to say nothing of the multiple pleasures it provides.

We read ourselves into literature without concern, as we are in science, for whether or not it is true for others, and if so, for how many and to what degree. Instead, the truth of any literary expression is immediately true for the reader because it corresponds to his or her experience or provides a language for it in a way that had not been available before. We say, "that is true for me, true to my own experience." This is my story. That's exactly the way I felt. Or I had not realized its truth until I saw it on the page. That is what a good book is all about. At their best they bring insight, understanding, wonder, pleasure and yes, friendship. The encounter becomes a process of coming to a deeper understanding of those larger truths of reality that are often difficult to grasp in any other way. In the final analysis, then, that is the great appeal of literature for me, the reasons I am so strongly drawn to it now.

What is the value of this personal account? Does it any meaning for someone other than myself? Essentially I am asking about the generality of my account? Are other readers drawn to literature for similar reasons? Could my experience be useful in promoting reading among the increasing number of non-readers? All too many bemoan the decline of reading in this country, but all too few of these commentators having any suggestions for overcoming it. Perhaps my experience has some relevance in confronting this problem. I realize it is presumptuous of me to say this. But who does not wish to better understand themselves or to see themselves depicted on the page? Who can turn away from a character who thinks and feels the same way as you or who helps you to clarify your thinking or spark your hope? This has been my experience in reading literature and I suspect it often is for other readers, as well.

Marks in the Margin

> *Time was when readers kept commonplace books. Whenever they came across a pithy passage, they copied it into a notebook under an appropriate heading...Reading and writing were therefore inseparable activities. They belonged to a continuous effort to make sense of things.*
>
> Robert Darnton

Reading great works of literature is not one I want to forget. So from the beginning of my reading days, I have been recording the notable passages that I come across in the books and periodicals I read. My collection of these passages has grown to several volumes during the almost thirty years since I have been adding to it. Following a long established tradition, the collection is known as my Commonplace Book.

When I come across something notable that I have read, I put a little mark by it in the margin or enclose the relevant passage in parentheses. I invariably stop to think about it for a moment before adding the page number on which it appears to a list I keep on the inside back cover of the book or last page of whatever periodical I am reading. Once I've finished the material, I copy each of the passages that I've marked in a word document on my computer.

I know some people feel differently about this, that the meaning of a passage can only be fully grasped by copying them by hand. But because I write so poorly the computer has made it possible for me to record these passages in a readable form with ease. I can't imagine having a volume of such length, or of any length for that matter, were it not for my laptop, nor that I would continue the practice so avidly without giving it a second thought.

Some of the books I read have a great many marked passages, others very few. I used to judge the quality of a book by the number of passages that I've marked. Eventually I realized that was a mistake, since occasionally I come across a really worthwhile book in which I don't mark any passages. At the end of each year, I make a copy of the collected passages and add them to my ever-growing Commonplace Book.

Recently a friend wrote to me that she also keeps such a book, one that is not so much a record of her reading but rather of certain ideas that come up in the enormous number of books she reads. She believed the passages fell into some kind of pattern that she was trying to understand. My hunch is that she will spend a lifetime at this thankless task. She also said she would kill herself if she lost it.

In the beginning my Commonplace Book was largely composed of quotations that struck me as worth recording for one reason or another. The first entry is from Samuel Coleridge: *Advice is like snow; the softer it falls...the deeper it sinks into the mind.* The idea has considerable appeal to me now, although I'm not sure why it did at the time I made note of it. Soon after there is one from William James: *Wisdom is learning what to overlook.* Again the notion has grown in meaning over the years. Eventually the entries became longer.

> *When they ask me, as of late they frequently do, how I have for so many years continued an equal interest in medicine and the poem, I reply that they amount for me to nearly the same thing.* —William Carlos Williams.

> *At the breakfast table I always open the newspaper to the sports page first. The sports page records people's accomplishments. The front page has nothing but men's failures.* —George Plimpton.

Then I began to split apart the quotations from a miscellaneous collection of phrases and short extracts that I called Briefs. These could be anything from an amusing phrase or word, a sentence from the *New York Times*, a periodical, or something I read on the web:

> *Eat! You need strength to worry.* — Jewish Fortune Cookie message.

> *The whole world seemed to have changed into a Robert Altman movie. Jarring and sour and crazy and colored in a palette that I believe drove my entire generation mildly insane.* —Michael Chabon.

Soon I begin to separate the Quotes and Briefs from the Passages that comprised the longer sections I began to copy from the books and periodicals that I was reading. For example, I copied several memorable passages from Ian McEwan's *Atonement*:

> *...the strangeness of the here and now, of what passed between people, the ordinary people that she knew, and what power one could have over the other, and how easy it was to get everything wrong, completely wrong.*
>
> *...nothing was ever as one imagined it.*
>
> *The age of clear answers was over.*
>
> *Whatever humble nursing she did, and however well or hard she did it, whatever illumination in tutorial she had relinquished, or lifetime moment on a college law, she would never undo the damage. She was unforgivable.*

Each year my Commonplace Book consists of entries in each of these groups with the Passages by far the largest of the three sections. In 2004 I added thirty-seven pages of Passages and four pages of Briefs and since I entered only a few new quotations I did not print a new Quotes section that year.

By way of comparison, in 1996, the first year that I began to distinguish the three types of entries, there were eleven pages of Passages, four of Briefs, and two of Quotes. This difference can be attributed to the fact I now have far more time for reading than I did in the nineties when I was still actively engaged in teaching and research. Beginning in 2002 the number of Passages increased almost twofold compared to previous years. I have no idea why this occurred. There was also a further doubling during the next four years so in 2005, I recorded fifty-five pages of Passages. I think these changes are due largely to the improving quality of the books I am reading now. After all, one can only read so many romance novels.

Reading serious literature takes time. To make the most of it a reader should be able to linger over the text for a while, pause to give it some thought, stop to mark a memorable passage, and perhaps revisit it before moving on. Ideally a reader should be free of the distractions of pressing work deadlines, household chores, or other responsibilities and be able to disengage from the onslaught of the media, phone, and the Internet. These are the conditions of my life now. It is also true that I've taken a liking to the practice of commonplacing; it has become a habit as well as a commitment to maintain a record of the noteworthy ideas that I have found on the pages of the literary works that I've been fortunate enough to read.

In a recent interview at Salon.com James Salter asserted: *"Sentences should not cause you to stop and admire them. They should be in the service of the page."* That brought me to a halt and I proceeded to do the very thing Salter said I shouldn't. After pondering his claim for a bit, I began to wonder if I should give up the practice required to maintain my Commonplace Book. Am I missing the sheer power of the page by stopping to admire a sentence or make note of one from time to time? Have I lost sight of why I began copying extracts in the first place and the inherent benefits of the practice? These questions more or less answered themselves, for in stopping to consider Salter's claim I was thoroughly in the "service of the page." It was not the sentence *per se* that caused me to stop. Rather, I stopped because of the effect the sentence had on me and the way it led me to want to make special note of its meaning and consider, for a moment, the several questions it raised.

Recently I've begun to wonder what it would it be like if I stopped recording passages. Could I do that? Would my reading experience be any different? The questions are not unlike those a person might ask who wishes to change a very strong habit. In a word, it wouldn't be easy. Marking and then recording the memorable passages in the books I read has become central to my reading experience. I usually stop reading a book when it doesn't engage me in this fashion. And so to discontinue the practice would make reading a far less absorbing experience than it has become for me.

I suspect many readers make little marks in the books they read. It seems a natural thing to do. Yet only a few readers that I know keep a record of these passages. A few years ago I learned that the practice began in antiquity and that it achieved considerable prominence during the Renaissance. Yet I was completely unaware of the tradition at the time I started my own collection. The fact that I, along with other readers, keep a commonplace book without knowing about this centuries old practice suggests it reflects a rather fundamental feature of the reading experience.

Frankly, I am not at all sure why I began the practice in the first place. The passages must have stood out for one reason or another and I may have wanted to make a record of them in order to reread them sometime in the future. I think I also had dreams of doing some writing. I know I admired a great many writers and often wondered how they were able to write so well. In my naïve way, I must have imagined that if I studied their works carefully and copied portions of them often enough, I might one day be able to write like they did.

In thinking back to the origins of my Commonplace Book, I realize now I must have found something in the literature I was reading that was not only different but was also somehow more truthful, more discerning about what truly mattered in my life than what I was reading in psychology. I don't recall collecting passages in the academic books and journals I was reading. Yes, I took notes but those were for my lectures and classroom presentations and were never added to my Commonplace Book or preserved in special notebooks. I may have placed them in a file for the next time I taught the class but not because I found them memorable or otherwise worth saving because they were especially significant.

Lately, I have begun to think of my Commonplace Book as a form of collecting; in my case, collecting ideas as well as clever or provocative expressions that stand apart from ordinary discourse and are, for that reason, worth preserving. In some cases they serve as a standard against which to judge my own attempts to write with some degree of clarity. Collecting ideas also has a number of distinct advantages compared to collecting most other objects—they cost next to nothing, they are easy to find, do not clutter up your closet, and don't require periodic repair or maintenance.

I've been keeping my commonplace book for over 25 years, 27 to be exact as of 2015. In it, I've recorded passages in all of the books I've read and once in a while an essay or article. The collection is enormous, page after page of reflections, random thoughts, questions, and sentences. All of them sit quietly on my computer that would otherwise consist of several thousand, double sided, single spaced pages.

Whenever I tell someone about my commonplace book, I'm usually told they've never heard of the idea. And then many vow to start keeping one of their own. I've no idea how many of them actually begin their own collection

At other times I am asked why I even bother to make note of passages in the books I read. I answer it is simply part of the reading experience, the way I began reading and continued in all the years of my education and teaching. Some people take photos to preserve their day-to-day experiences; I mark and then record passages in the books I read to preserve mine.

I read a sentence of a paragraph and stop to think about it. But it seems that isn't enough. Something more, a physical response is required. So I mark the passages with a pen and often write about them on the keyboard. That too is a natural part of the way I read. The entire sequence of reading, marking and then recording is bound up together, each one dependent on the other, incomplete without all three.

I often wonder what to do with all the passages. Once in a while I read a random page or two and am immediately struck by how many remarkable passages there are. A few years ago I did undertake a study of the most frequent categories in what was then volume one but that was relatively informal analysis, carried out by the very person who selected the passages in the first place. The bias that can intrude on such a study is obvious.

Yet the large collection of passages is a gold mine. Every time I turn to it, the wisdom of the assembled collection cannot be denied. Here and there, I come across a sentence, a paragraph that suggests something more general, something to write about, ponder.

How can these nuggets remain locked away on the pages of an unknown, idiosyncratic scribe of the late 20th and early 21st century? How to mine this wealth? At first I think a statistical analysis would be the easiest. I soon realize that isn't going to capture the meanings of the passages, some obvious but most second or third order concepts. Nor their beauty.

I go through some pages and start my own analysis. It takes forever, although it is worth it. Perhaps I can find someone to help me, someone who knows a little about me and my reading proclivities. A volunteer appears. She starts, develops an interesting taxonomy, but soon gives up. It is too much for her. I am not surprised.

It is too much for the software. Too much for the volunteer. No doubt it is too much for me, but I start.

I begin with the pages for 2010. At once I am halted by two passages that hit home:

From the poet William Carlos Williams:

> *Whether we're young, or we're all grown up and just starting out, or we're getting old, or getting so old there's not much time left, we're looking for company, and we're looking for understanding: someone who reminds us that we're not alone and someone who wonders out loud about things that happen in this life, the way we do when we're walking or sitting or driving and thinking things over.*

From Paul Auster's *Paris Review* Interview:

> *Time begins slipping away, and simple arithmetic tells you there are more years behind you than ahead of you—many more. Your body starts breaking down, you have aches and pains that weren't there before, and little by little the people you love begin to die. By the age of fifty, most of us are haunted by ghosts. They live inside us and we spend as much time talking to the dead as to the living. It's hard for a young person to understand this. It's not that a twenty year old doesn't know he's going to die, but it's the loss of others that so profoundly affects an older person—and you can't know what the accumulation of losses is going to do to you until you experience it yourself.*

It continues like this, slowly. Occasionally I come across a book I don't recall. I know I read it; the copied passages are the evidence. But I cannot recall a single thing about its story or characters. This happens from time to time, even though my memory is fully operational. I go to find the book on the shelf. Of course, it isn't there. This happens all too often.

I continue and come across the passages from an article I do recall reading. It suggests a game, one for which there is no app. I call the game Counterfactuals.

One way to think about what a work of art does is to imagine the counterfactual—how would my life have been different had I not spent the last three months reading War and Peace? The answers, I think tend to group into three categories: The social experiences I had because of the book; the ideas the book incorporated into my life; and the aesthetic moments that were opened to me because of what I was reading.

I start playing the game with the book I just finished, *The Spinoza Problem*, by Irvin Yalom. Immediately a counterfactual comes to mind.

But I am distracted by all of this. What to do with these gems remains?

Journey Through the Book

Culture is not only passed on orally or by instinctive imitation, but above all through reading and study, hence also through the assistance of such a small object as a bookmark.

Marco Ferreri

While only a few readers place marks in the margin by the notable passages they find on the page, almost all mark their place in a book in some fashion when they put the book down. I had forgotten about the special nature of this practice until from out of the blue a friend recently sent me a beautiful book on the subject of bookmarks—Marco Ferreri's *Bookmarks*. What an unusual subject for a book, I thought. The small volume is much like a catalogue that you would find at a museum. In fact, it was published in conjunction with a bookmark exhibition held in Milan a few years ago that was organized by Italian furniture manufacturer.

Again I thought how strange that seemed—what do bookmarks have to do with manufacturing furniture? However, the author assured me that a furniture manufacturer's interest in bookmarks should not appear the least bit odd by pointing out that the tables and chairs that his firm makes are closely associated with the act of reading and studying, both of which require that a bookmark be close at hand. Who can deny such impeccable logic?

Each page of the book displays a collection of bookmarks reproduced in their approximate size and color and organized around a common theme—bookshops, publishers, cinemas, propaganda, cosmetics, etc. I had no idea there were so many different varieties of bookmarks or that they were often crafted with such artistic skill. The book is a work of art in itself and it started me mulling over the role that bookmarks in my own reading life and then, the more I dwelled on it, what they mean for readers in general.

I don't know if you are, but I'm very particular about the bookmarks I use. They have to be just the right size. I don't like small ones like the business cards or bus tickets that some readers use; they tend to fall out of books or get lost somewhere, so they are really quite useless. I don't much care for paper clips that crease the pages of books I am reading or those printed on flimsy paper that tear or bend easily.

The bookmarks at Powell's in Portland, Oregon said to be one of the world's largest, used to be like that. I never liked them at all and always just put them in my recycling box whenever I found one in a book I had purchased there. But Mr. Powell must have taken to heart comparable stories from his many loyal customers for just recently I noticed he has stiffened up his bookmarks so that they now remain in the books I buy there rather than on the stack of papers in my recycling box.

One of my favorite bookmarks is given out by a small, independent bookstore in Portland that I've been going to for almost 40 years. It is a miracle the store is still in business given the likes of Amazon.com and the crowd at Borders and Barnes & Noble. The store is called Twenty-Third Avenue Books, and they have an almost perfect bookmark, one that has remained the same during all the years that I've been going there. They keep doling them out from an inventory that must number in the millions.

Sadly, the store has recently closed, only to be replaced by a yoghurt store. Such is the story of many small, independent bookstores. Fortunately, I saved every bookmark they gave me. They are just the right size, about five inches long, and just the right texture, firm and not easily bent. Their address and phone number is printed on one side, while on the others is a quote by A. Edward Newton: *"The buying of more books than one can read is nothing less than the soul reaching toward...infinity."* Nothing fancy, just the basics, along with a suggestion about how to help them stay in business. I am also partial to their bookmarks because I still recall the bookish atmosphere in the store and the kindly people who worked there.

Some of the books I like to read are reviewed in *The New York Times* or one of the other literary publications I've been reading lately. If it is thoughtful analysis, I will print a copy, fold it into bookmark shape and keep it to use as a bookmark in my copy of the book. This makes a dandy bookmark, one that I can review from time to time as I read the book. Not colorful or the least bit artistic, but definitely informative, as well as functional. I seem to be using them more and more lately, which is too bad for all the bookmark artists and printers hard at work at their trade.

Every now and then I read a book that is a treasure. Some of these are reference books, like the dictionary or encyclopedia. Others are books of paintings or photographs. These books clearly require one of the cherished bookmarks that I've collected over the years in my travels. These usually turn out to be made of thin leather with a calligraphed message or distinctive symbol printed on the front side. Or they might already include one those colorful ribbon strips that sometimes accompany those really fine and important books, as well as all my red Michelin guides of hotels and restaurants in Italy and France.

These narrow cloth or silk ribbons that are bound into the book at the top of the spine are said to be the eighteenth and nineteenth century precursors of the modern bookmark. It is a mystery why they aren't included in every book. Wonder of wonders, the *Paris Review* now includes a bookmark with each issue. Such a simple idea--promote the periodical, aid those who take their time reading the material, point the way to the publisher's website where the reader can search the archive, listen to poems, and by golly also subscribe. Then again, maybe it is not such a good idea, since if it is widely adopted it will pretty much be the end of bookmark craftsman, as well as the pleasure of collecting distinctive bookmarks.

I keep my most valued bookmarks in a very special box upon my desk. My wife, who knows all too well how keen I am about nifty boxes, gave it to me on my birthday one year. The box is about the size of an egg carton that opens with a hinged lid and has always sat upon my desk ever since I received it. It has more than enough room to house all my favorite bookmarks. The lid is appropriately calligraphed with passages about writing. *Writing is nothing more than a guided dream* (Jorge Luis Borges). *If there's a book you really want to read, but it hasn't been written yet, then you must write it* (Toni Morrison). *True ease in writing comes from art not chance* (Proust).

Most of the special bookmarks that I place in this box are from Italy, some from Oxford and a couple that I still have from the Library of Congress. I also keep at least one from my favorite bookstores—Keplers in Menlo Park, Cody's in Berkeley, Blackwells in London, WH Smith in Paris and Powells, just down the block from my home. I also keep one made by the publisher of a little book of essays that I wrote. This bookmark has a blurb about the book and a photograph of me with my cat Ernie sitting on my shoulders. Silly isn't it? These books do more than allow me to mark my place in a book. They also set loose a string of associations of the place I visited, who I was with, what the weather was like and what I did when I was there or, in the case of the bookmark for my recent book, the pleasure I had in writing those essays.

One of the principal rules of bookmarking is that the book and its bookmark must be suitably matched. You wouldn't want to use a bookmark from Twenty Third Avenue Books in the Second Edition of the *American Heritage Dictionary* or the *Collected Photographs of Edward Steichen*. Books like those call for one of those special leather bookmarks with calligraphed text and striped bottom edge.

I've asked a few of my reader friends if they have any special preference about the bookmarks they use. One reported she uses any old item that happens to be hanging around like an old postcard, Polaroid, or food stamp pamphlet. Another wrote to me that she never leaves a bookstore without checking to see if they have a bookmark to add to her rather enormous collection. She reported that aside from bookstores, her best finds are in museums. She is also particular about her bookmarks noting that she doesn't really like the metal or plastic versions because they don't feel quite right. Who wants to keep a lump of metal in the middle of a book?

A variety of bookmarks have made an appearance in works of literature. Louse in Graham Greene's *The Heart of the Matter* was said to be an avid reader who used *"hairpins, inside the library books where she had marked her place."* Christine the professor In Tessa Hadley's short story, *Mother's Son*, used a widely employed bookmarking technique: *"...books by Rhys and Woolf and Bowen were piled all around her, some of them open face down on the table, some of them bristling with torn bits of papers as bookmarks."*

More recently, and to my relief, the art of bookmarking has been restored to its aesthetic integrity by Michael Ondaatje in *Divisadero*: *"Once Lucien picked up a book that the thief had been reading and saw a sprig of absinthe leaves used as a bookmark. That felt like the only certain thing about the man, and from then on, every few days, the writer carefully noted the progress of the absinthe, making its own journey through the plot."*

The other day I asked my wife, a voracious reader, if she had thought much about the place of bookmarks in her reading life. She replied quite simply that she never uses a bookmark with the clear implication that my question was pretty stupid. I thought that odd at the time until I realized she usually reads a book from start to finish in a single session, so obviously she would have no need for anything as mundane as a bookmark. Neither did my aunt who I recalled the other day used to tear each page out of a book once she had finished reading it. What a booklover she was! Of course, I only saw her do that when she was reading cheap paperback novels. Since I never saw her reading anything else, I doubt if she ever had need for anything as humdrum as a bookmark.

On the other hand, another reader friend of mine reports that she has a special fondness for bookmarks largely because she often makes her own. She recounted several such occasions when she was at the beach with her daughter and grandchildren. The bookmarks they made that day included glued shells, sand and seagull feathers. It was a good memory for her. Another was a time when she was sitting around with some close friends and someone suggested they make bookmarks for one another. She still has a couple of those and every time she uses one they remind her of some special people and the times they were together.

Recently I have adopted the practice of ordering some of my books from Amazon. I don't always like doing that because it comes at the expense of my favorite local bookshops. But Amazon is quick, and convenient, and I don't have to suit up in the winter to go over to Powells. Amazon almost always has a new copy of every book I want and then some.

In the old days Amazon used to send me an attractive bookmark along with each order.

They were made of firm paper, colorfully decorated, were a goodly length (8 inches), with a booklover's quote on one side. Here are a few examples:

> *A book is like a garden carried in the pocket.* (Chinese Proverb).
>
> *When I get a little money I buy books; and if any is left I buy food and clothes* (Erasmus).
>
> *The test of literature is, I suppose, whether we ourselves live more intensely for the reading of it* (Elizabeth Drew).
>
> *When you sell a man a book, you don't sell him 12 ounces of paper and ink and glue—you sell him a whole new life* (Christopher Morley).

A few years ago Amazon stopped including bookmarks with my order. That was unfortunate. I still have every one they sent me housed in my box of favorite bookmarks. I wonder why they stopped the practice? I must e-mail Jeff Bezos to find out. He has become one of my virtual friends and I often send him an e-mail. But instead of attractive bookmarks, he now sends me a traveling coffee mug each Christmas. Quite frankly, I'd prefer a bookmark with an expression that reminds me how lucky I am to be able to read the books in the packages that he sends.

I have been going to Italy a great deal lately. I don't know exactly why except that I have come to feel at home there and rather taken with the life and beauty that surrounds me. Most of the time I stay in Florence where I rent an apartment for a month or two. Over the years, I have discovered all the English language bookstores in the Centro, some of which rival anything you might find in this country or England. Each one has its own bookmark that has been duly added to my collection. But mostly I've been accumulating those with beautiful pictures of the Tuscan landscape. They are just the right size, printed on heavy paper with a photograph in the center-- a field of sunflowers, a villa in the distance, vines are hanging limp with grapes, the golden hillsides of Tuscany.

Along with its countless works of art and historical monuments, Florence is also known a center for printing fine paper. One of the most renowned printers is the Bottega d'Arte Guilio Ginnini & Figlio. They have designed a distinctive tri-fold bookmark that describes in four languages their fine paper products including sheets of paper salvaged from the books that were irreparably damaged in the great Florentine flood of 1966. It is not surprising that this has become one of my most cherished bookmarks, also housed quite naturally in my special bookmark box.

Bookmarks have not escaped the wonders of the digital age either. A 21st Century reader can now purchase a digital bookmark with a built in dictionary, the ever-popular Selco Bookmark Dictionary II. It is said to hold 130,000 words with "definitions thoroughly revised and updated." They can be had at Amazon.com for a little over $35. Whoever heard of paying for a bookmark? The "keypad" of this gadget is no thicker than your ordinary bookmark. However, it is attached at the top to a modest-size LCD screen that not only displays the meaning of words, but when it is not in the dictionary mode, also the date and time of day for readers who can't live without this information. There is a scrolling feature for those wordy definitions, plus key for viewing the previous definition. As if that is not enough, it also incorporates a calculator for readers who are trying to solve Fermant's Last Theorem. I have been rendered speechless by the thing. The screen sits up upon the top of the keypad, like Humpty-Dumpty on his wall. I have a feeling it won't be long before my jazzy new Selco Bookmark Dictionary II will experience a similar fate.

For readers who are ready to upgrade to a five-star deluxe bookmark, I can report that Tiffany's new bamboo leaf/scarab bookmark in sterling silver is now available. I saw it advertised in *the Times* the other day and was duly informed it is designed for bookmark lovers who want to add a touch of glamour to their favorite coffee-table book. Each one is carefully embossed with bamboo stalks and a tiny cooper and gold beetle. At $120 it would make a perfect Christmas gift for all your bookish friends. You don't live near a Tiffany store? No problem, just go to their online store to order this gem. Better do so before they run out; I am sure the supply is limited.

Recently the Internet has recently given birth to new meaning for the word "bookmark." Now there are digital bookmarks to accompany all those "real world" versions that have given readers such pleasure over the centuries. If you asked someone today to describe a bookmark, they are likely to tell you it is one of their favorite websites that can be reached by clicking on its link in the browser they are using. Of course, there is nothing aesthetically appealing about these kinds of bookmarks, nor does their appearance vary in any particular respect. They are surely not going to be collected or treasured like the bookmarks of yesteryear and no one is going to get very choosy about how they look or feel either either.

It bothers me a bit to dilute the meaning of an object that is as richly valued as a bookmark that we use in reading a book. So I have been thinking it might really be a good idea to think of another way to refer to the Web pages that we want to remember. How about webmark, virtualmark or digimark? Any of those terms would do. Don't they denote more accurately what a Web site is than the word "bookmark does?"

There is even a site on the Web now devoted exclusively to the topic of bookmarks. While not the most popular site on the Web (Since February 2001, it has had over 21,000 "visitors.") if you go to www.miragebookmark.ch/index.html you'll find links to a sizeable number of bookmark collections and exhibitions, documents on the history of bookmarks and information about exchanging books with other collectors. You could also visit a site on how to make bookmarks, as well as a host of other web-shops to purchase them. In fact, recently I did a bookmark search on www.ebay.com and to my amazement discovered there were over 12 pages displaying more that 575 bookmark collections that you could bid on there. Who would have believed that the world of bookmarks is so vast?

The beautiful book of the bookmark exhibition in Milan set the occasion for my ramblings about this world. I'm not quite sure why it did. But once I started, it was not difficult to keep going. And in doing so, I began to appreciate that bookmarks are not just for marking a page in the books I am reading. To be sure I want them to do that, but I also want them to do the job reliably, that is, I don't want them to fall out or bend easily or be so flimsy that they quickly begin to crumble.

Yes, it never hurts if they are also aesthetically pleasing or informative in some way, say by including a memorable passage about reading by a well-known writer, or a thoughtful review of the book I am reading. It is no less important that they be worth preserving for some reason.

I don't collect a great many objects. I may save a few postcards from places I have been in my travels or photographs of the special people in my life or treasures that someone has made for me. But that's about it. Except, of course, for the bookmarks from my favorite bookstores.

Each of the treasured bookmarks in my little box conjures up a memory of the bookstore, the town where it is located, its size, quality of its collection, the light in the store and the feeling that comes to me when I am there. In this sense a bookmark is indistinguishable from any memento, say a photograph or a trinket from a place I have been.

Both seek to preserve an experience that was in some way memorable and don't want to forget. For my friend who makes them it is the memories of some people who helped her construct them. For me it is primarily the memories of the good times I have had in the places where I found them. In this way, a bookmark does its part, albeit a small one, to sustain the culture of reading and all that follows from that experience.

Annotating Ian McEwan's Saturday

The key word for the commonplace book is "annotated." It is not just an anthology; the compiler reacts to the passages he has chosen or tells what the passages have led him to think about. A piece of prose, a poem, an aphorism can trigger the mind to consider a parallel, to dredge something from the memory, or perhaps to speculate with further range and depth on the same theme.

William Cole

I marked forty-five separate passages in Ian McEwan's *Saturday*, an intellectually rich novel about a single day in the life of Henry Perowne, a British neurosurgeon. As is my practice and that of most other readers who keep a commonplace book, I did not annotate those selections at the time they were recorded. However, I paused to give some thought to many of them and have expanded upon those considerations in this essay.

Henry Perowne is a deeply reflective man. He muses, ruminates, broods and wonders about one thing or another--the nature of his discipline, his family, the routine chores that occupy his day, and the troublesome times in which he lives during the early years of the 21st century. The changing conditions of the contemporary world are a constant worry, as is the apparent decline of Western values and ideals. McEwan describes *"the drift, the white noise of [Perowne's] solitary thought"* and at one point characterizes his state as a *"folly of over-interpretation."*

In turn, I was led to ponder his musings and the extent to which I agreed with them or not. As a result, although it was not a very lengthy novel, it took me forever to read—a pleasure devoutly treasured by this reader. McEwan speculates a good deal about the sources of human behavior and difficulties of identifying them with any precision. Since I have been concerned with those very same issues throughout my professional life, I marked a goodly number where McEwan writes about them.

Parental Influence

> *It's a commonplace of parenting and modern genetics that parents have little or no influence on the characters of their children. You never know who you are going to get. Opportunities, health, prospects, accent, table manners—these might lie within your power to shape.*

I have come to believe that the influence of parents on their children is subtler than McEwan implies here. To be sure, you can never predict the outcome of your children's early experiences or their genetic heritage. But that, in itself, is not grounds for concluding parents have little influence on their children.

We hear much doubt expressed today about the direct impact of parents on their children's personality and adult behavior, indeed, whether or not they matter at all or matter as much as their peers. It is said, for example, that parental influence on their children has been overestimated. Studies of identical twins (reared apart or together) are cited to show that genetic factors control about a half of a person's intellect and personality. Other studies of fatherless children are said to be consistent with this evidence. Rearing a child without an adult male in the household appears to have very little *particular* impact on children. Instead, factors associated with income, frequency of moving, and peer relationships are said to matter more.

My own feeling is that these claims say less about the influence of parents on their children and far more about the methods used to obtain the evidence, especially the methods used to assess adult behavior and personality. Frankly, I do not believe these methods tap the important dimensions of human personality and intellectual ability. Nor do I think the findings have a very high degree of generality

I also believe whatever influence parents have on their children is not likely to be very specific. Instead, their influence has much more to do with very general personality and character dimensions rather than specific behaviors, table manners included. We learn from our parents *very general aspects of character and motivation*. We learn to value learning, not any particular discipline. We see what it means to be generous and helpful, not any particular instance of these acts. In short, our parents provide exemplars for those deeper aspects of human character and feeling that find are expressed in the sort of person we become.

Genetic Control

> *But what really determines the sort of person who's coming to live with you is which sperm finds which egg, how the cards in the two packs are chosen, then how they are shuffled, halved and spliced at the moment of recombination. Cheerful or neurotic, kind or greedy, curious or dull, expansive or shy and anywhere in between; it can be quite an affront to parental self-regard, just how much of the work has already been done.*

No one can deny the powerful impact of genetic factors on personality and behavior, although the fine details of how this occurs remain a mystery. Still, to say that genes are *"what really determines the sort of person who's coming to live with you"* goes well beyond the evidence. It is a truism to say they interact and work in combination with environmental factors.

The real advances in our knowledge will come from determining the mechanism whereby genes exert their control and whether or not this mechanism is modifiable or reversible. We cannot change a person's eye color, but we may be able to alter other characteristics that are under genetic control, such as height, weight and the risk of certain diseases. In such cases, well known diet, exercise, and general lifestyle patterns can be decisive.

I recall an early experiment in behavior genetics. Two strains of rats can be breed over successive generations that differ markedly in their aggressiveness, with one strain highly aggressive in the presence of another rat and the other very non-aggressive in the same situation. However, these differences can be completely reversed by varying their early rearing experiences.

When an aggressive strain is reared in the presence of other rats, they no longer attack other rats in adulthood. However, if this strain is raised in isolation, they continue to behave aggressively as adults. On the other hand, when the non-aggressive strain is raised in isolation, they become extremely aggressive as adults in the presence of other rats. But they do not behave this way if they are reared in a social situation.

In a word, some forms of behavior normally thought to be under genetic control can be modified and completely reversed under appropriate environmental conditions. This finding is not restricted to aggressive behavior or to rats. The principle has been demonstrated to hold with other behaviors and other species, including humans. There is, indeed, far more to determining *"what really determines the sort of person"* your child will be than the random meeting of two eggs.

Neurophysiological Effects

McEwan is clearly interested in many other current issues confronting the study of human behavior. Indeed, there are several long sections in *Saturday* that treat in highly technical and at times chilling language various neurophysiological diseases and the surgical procedures that Perowne employs in attempting to restore normal brain function. I did not make note of any of these passages, largely because they were well beyond my comprehension. But if I was a neuroscientist I might have. However, I did note one passage concerning chemical factors governing the transmission of nerve impulses.

> *Who could ever reckon up the damage done to love and friendship and all hopes of happiness by a surfeit or depletion of this or that neurotransmitter?*

For years I have pondered the mystery of my father's illness, the alternating cycles of depression and elation that governed his life. I wondered what was at work to give rise to this strange and sad mix of horrible and wonderful days. I have read countless accounts of the relationship between brain chemistry and this malady and the way it can sometimes be corrected by drugs that counteract whatever neurotransmitter malfunction exists to give an individual some relief, sometimes total relief, from its symptoms.

But all this has never really helped me to better understand his torments. Neither psychoanalytic therapy, the drugs available at that time, electroshock treatment, or the best private "rest homes," gave him any lasting relief. Would the newer drugs and treatments available today have made a difference? Perhaps they might have made it easier for him to manage the furies more effectively or put them at a greater distance.

However, I am not at all sure about this and I remain a skeptic about the current views of the brain mechanisms that may be responsible for what is now known as bi-polar disorder. Yes, he may have had some kind of chemical imbalance, but I saw the world in which he grew up, the way his mother and father treated him, and how he had to spend his working days in the family business. It was never a placid situation. There was no escaping the world he brought with him but neither could he escape the one he had to live through during each and every day of his relatively brief life.

Non-verbal Behavior

In several sections of *Saturday* Perowne mulls over the significance of the odd quirks of his patients and those he encounters during the course of that day. For example, the moment he sees Baxter, the driver of the car he bumped into, Perowne senses something about him is not quite right. He notes at once signs of *"poor self control, emotional lability, explosive temper suggestive of reduced levels of GABA among the appropriate binding sites on striatal neurons."*

Perowne is truly a diagnostician of the first order. I made note of other passages in which McEwan ponders the meaning of non-verbal behaviors, including the following one:

> *But can anyone really know the sign, the tell of an honest man? There's been some good work on this very question. Perowne has read Paul Ekman on the subject. In the smile of a self-conscious liar certain muscle groups in the face are not activated. They*

only come to life as the expression of genuine feeling. The smile of a deceiver is flawed, insufficient.

It seems that at almost every moment of waking life, we attempt to make inferences about other individuals based on incomplete knowledge or unreliable indicators. Often I wonder what can you tell about a person by the e-mails they write? Are they telling the truth or performing before you in this medium? Does the message reflect their authentic self, the one you would encounter if you met them?

Here I think the issue is not so much the authenticity of the e-mailer but rather the accuracy of the attribution process. How often I have been struck by the discrepancy between the picture I have of an e-mail correspondent whom I have yet to meet and the reality of the person once we do eventually come face to face.

A person once told me they were charmed by the words in my e-mails but that the real me was not the least bit appealing. And in an essay on an online relationship she had formed, Megham Daum writes *"...though we both knew that the "me" in his mind consisted largely of himself... I was horrified by the realization that I had invested so heavily in a made-up character ..."* She was somewhat taken aback when she finally met the person she had been e-mailing for months and notes that if she had met him at a party she would have scarcely spoken to him.

To the best of my knowledge no one has investigated the accuracy of perceptions formed from e-mail messages. I find the issue fascinating and because it is so commonplace now, I am sure it will be examined before too long. Here the question is really no different that determining the truth of what another person says on the basis of their facial expression or the way they express themselves in ordinary language as conveyed by the words they write on their keyboard. People vary widely in the style and manner they write e-mails and this must surely be related to other aspects of their personality and character.

Scientific Truth

In *Saturday* and elsewhere McEwan has expressed his optimism about the ability of science to unravel the mysteries of the brain and the truth about consciousness. There are several passages in Saturday that deal with general matters of scientific inquiry and method. I was especially struck by this succinct remark.

> ...*statistical probabilities are not the same as truths.*

This claim is at the heart of the disenchantment I began to experience with the work I was doing in psychology. Psychologists seek to establish very general laws of human thought and action. Yet I never understood how evidence derived by averaging the scores of a group of individuals could serve as the foundation for a science of *individual* behavior.

Laws based on such aggregate data tell us very little about specific individuals and serve only to obscure crucial features of human variability and uniqueness. Further, the many exceptions to these laws severely limits their generality. Thus, it is impossible to say with much confidence that they hold for a particular individual at a particular time and place.

This conclusion is not unlike one often voiced in judicial proceedings, where the legal standing of psychological research is also called into question. It took me a while to understand why courts were so hesitant to admit social science evidence, let alone take it seriously in adjudicating cases. Yet legal cases are decided on an *individual* basis and so, even when the weight of evidence clearly supports the relevant social science generalization, the courts still require "proof" that it applies in the case being adjudicated.

When judges ask psychologists to link the general principle to the specific case, it is difficult, if not impossible for them to do so with certainty. But that is what the law requires. Psychologists can provide relevant case knowledge and guidance, but the information they present is rarely, if ever, decisive in judicial decision-making.

Similarly, I know enough about psychology to be wary of psychological generalizations and the statistical methods they are based on. You can never be entirely confident about the applicability of evidence derived from this approach. Psychology will always have to be content with this sort of limitation. Laws based on group means hold for some people, some of the time, but one never can be sure on any given occasion if they apply to a particular individual in the situation at hand.

Fortuitous Events

Random events play a key role in many of the situations described in Saturday.

The random combination of two embryonic eggs is said to determine a great deal about a person. The collision of the cars driven by Perowne and Baxter was a largely fortuitous event that might not have happened had either driver taken a different route or varied the speed they were driving. Elsewhere McEwan highlights the role of chance encounters in human events.

> *It troubles him to consider the powerful currents and fine turning that alter fates, the close and distant influences, the accidents of character and circumstance...*
>
> *The random ordering of the world, the unimaginable odds against any particular condition, still please him.*

Most accounts of personal change have neglected the powerful role of such events. One need only reflect on the major changes in their own life to realize the significance they have. When I ask students how their parents met, many report it was due to a chance meeting. One reported that his father was driving home from a business meeting and was involved in a serious automobile accident that required several weeks of hospital recuperation. The student's mother was his nurse and six months later they were married.

In a *New Yorker* profile, the late Yitzhak Rabin, former Prime Minister of Israel, described how he met his wife: *"It began with a chance encounter in a Tel Aviv street in 1944; a glance, a word, a stirring within and then a further meeting."*

Nancy Reagan, wife of the former President Ronald Reagan, experienced a similar turn of events. In response to her concern over the receipt of a series of mail announcements of Communist party meetings that were intended for another person with the same name, she sought the advice of Ronald Reagan, then president of the Screen Actors Guild. Not long after that they were married.

A chance encounter between two individuals is not a totally random event. Rather it is the intersection of their lawfully governed paths, like the meeting of two embryonic eggs or automobiles that can sometimes launch two individuals on entirely new path. Had the chance encounter not occurred, the two lives might have taken an entirely different course.

Social Change

> *No more big ideas. The world must improve, if at all, by tiny steps. People mostly take an existential view—having to sweep the streets for a living looks like simple bad luck. It's not a visionary age. The streets need to be cleaned.*

People often wonder why they should bother to vote when their vote doesn't matter anyway. Or they say ask why should they go to the trouble of taking the bus, when their attempt to save energy or reduce pollution in these ways isn't going to have the slightest effect on either of these problems.

Those who argue this way ignore a fundamental principle of social change. Although any single act has only a miniscule effect, the cumulative impact of each individual act can be quite substantial. For example, relatively modest energy savings at the individual level, say by turning down your thermostat or taking the bus once a week, can lead to considerable savings when combined with similar behaviors of a large number of other individuals.

The same is true for any situation that is influenced by the collective action of a large population of individuals. No one member of the population can determine the outcome of an election, but a large group of like-minded voters can. One need only recall recent elections in which candidates were victorious by margins of only one or two votes. If you voted for the winning candidate in this kind situation, it is clear that your vote made a difference. If you didn't vote for the losing candidate, again it is clear that your vote mattered. When taken together the individual actions of a small number of individual voters can influence the outcome of an election.

Individuals have to believe that what they do matters even though it is difficult for them to appreciate this in any real sense. Isn't one of the major issues then one of counteracting this widespread belief? Describing the tragedy of the commons might be one way. Imagine a group of herdsmen grazing their cattle on a common range. To increase their profits, each one is motivated to add a new animal to their herd. Since a herdsman will initially profit by doing so, each adds further animals to his herd. As a result, there is an inevitable increase in the total number of animals.

This leads very quickly to a serious overgrazing problem. The range is simply not adequate to support the increasing number of animals and, as its resources are gradually depleted, the animals in turn, are unable to survive. This eventually ends with the tragic ruin of all the herdsman.

Garrett Hardin has described such a situation as the "tragedy of commons" arguing that the logic of the commons operates whenever individuals have unlimited access to a cheap but finite resource. This logic dictates that through the rational actions of individuals pursuing their own well-being, the resources will inevitably be exploited until they can no longer support the population at large. Similarly, John Platt has characterized such situations as "social traps." He suggests that such traps occur when individuals, by pursuing their own self-interest, produce consequences that collectively are damaging to the group as a whole.

These concepts capture rather vividly the way in which the individual actions of a small group of individuals can influence a much larger population in the community. At the same time, they suggest how this logic can also be applied to the preservation of these resources. When the separate actions of individuals, say by driving less or using alternative transportation, are multiplied countless times over, year after year across a large number of individuals, their collective impact can be enormous.

In short, by thinking twice about their short-term interests, individuals can not only benefit the community as a whole but themselves as well. There is nothing glamorous about these actions or the least bit visionary, but little by little, with these "tiny steps" they will keep the air clearer and the gas flowing at the pumps.

Literary Experience

There is some discussion of literature in *Saturday* as Perowne's daughter is a poet and he is amused by her tutorials to try to get him up to speed about literary works. They have some delightful exchanges about his lack of interest in following her lead. And it is clear that Perowe is not much of a reader. So even though he is a deeply reflective man, I suppose one should not have been surprised, as I was at first, by the following passage

> *Henry read the whole of Anna Karenia and Madame Bovary, two acknowledged masterpieces. At the cost of slowing his mental processes and many hours of his valuable time, he committed himself to the shifting intricacies of these sophisticated fairy stories. What did he grasp after all? That adultery is understandable but wrong, that nineteenth-century women had a hard time of it, that Moscow and the Russian countryside and provincial France were once just so.*

Yet it was literature that saved the lives of Henry Perowne and his family in *Saturday*. It occurred in a dramatic incident when Perowne returns home after a harrowing day about the time the United States was about to launch its second war in Iraq. On the way to his early morning squash match, Perowne has a minor automobile collision with a person he senses at once is a criminal with an irreversible brain disease.

Later that day, Baxter, the criminal returns to Perowne's home to take revenge on him and those in this family who have gathered to welcome the return of Daisy. Baxter is holding a knife to Perowne's wife, Rosalind, and asks Daisy, whom he has told to strip, to read from her newly published book of poems. She is terrified, doesn't know if she can begin or what to read, and looks to her poet grandfather, Grammaticus, for a hint. He senses her dilemma and tells her to read the one she used to recite for him. Daisy catches the hint at once and begins reciting *Dover Beach*.

Baxter is transfixed by the beauty of the poem. *"You wrote that. You wrote that,"* he says in amazement. He asks her to read it again. When she is done reciting, Baxter's mood changes suddenly. He is thoroughly disarmed, overcome, as McEwan writes, by *"a yearning he could barely begin to define."* He removes the knife from Rosalind's neck, puts it back in his pocket, and tells his sidekick he has changed his mind. The tension is broken, the threat is over, and the overpowering of Baxter can begin.

Here, in the extreme is the power of literature.

> *Daisy recited a poem that cast a spell on one man. Perhaps any poem would have done the trick, and thrown the switch on a sudden mood change. Still, Baxter fell for the magic, he was transfixed by it, and he was reminded how much he wanted to live.*

The experience is not only the stuff of fiction. While not exactly a work of literature, reading from a book called *The Purpose-Driven Life* played a central role in saving the life of Ashley Smith, who, a few years ago, was held hostage for hours in her suburban apartment near Atlanta by Brian Nicholas, on the run after killing two people during his escape from a courthouse trial for an earlier murder. Smith claims that reading and speaking with Nicholas about the book gave her a chance to simply talk with him and begin the process of gaining his trust so that he would allow her to leave the apartment to see her daughter. Once out of the apartment, Smith called 911; Nicholas was captured moments later. Who knows what might have happened had she not been able to read sections of the book to Nicholas?

Waiting for The New Yorker

While the magazine certainly provided some readers with a symbolic city, others saw it as a bastion against the forces of cultural decline.

                                     Mary Corey

The New Yorker was as much a part of our class conditioning as clean fingernails, college, a checking account and good intentions. For better or worse, it probably created our sense of humor.

                                     John Leonard

The New Yorker magazine first drew me to the world of literature and fine writing. To this day and through all its recent transformations, it has continued to play a large role in my literary reading experiences. It is surely the most frequent single source of the entries in my Commonplace Book. I can't be entirely sure when I first started reading *The New Yorker*. Perhaps I was in high school or even younger. But I do recall there was always a copy around the house and I know that once I started reading the magazine, I never stopped. This is a tale told by most dedicated readers, including its current editor, David Remnick, who, upon assuming the post, remarked, "I was raised on this magazine."

What could the magazine have possibly meant to me as a young boy growing up in Los Angeles in the '40s and '50s? I know my mother read it from cover to cover each week, and surely I must have wondered what drew her to those pages with such devotion. No doubt I picked up a copy from time to time, glanced at the articles, and maybe read one of two, perhaps at her suggestion. And then as my education broadened in junior high and then high school, I remember reading sections of the magazine in earnest.

It became my Literature 101: a course that has lasted for years, indeed, to this day. And it introduced me to the cultural life of this country, at least as reflected in the goings on in New York. I became aware of the people who were profiled in the magazine, the heroes of high culture: the books they wrote and films they made or appeared in. I was taken away to worlds I never knew existed by the two or three short stories that were published then in each issue, and by those remarkable letters from foreign cities. What better introduction to Paris than those memorable "Letters from Paris" by Janet Flanner?

There was even a column on horse racing by Audax Minor, the pen name of George Ryall, which I read with considerable interest since it was not uncommon for my father to take us on the weekend to the thoroughbred races at Hollywood Park or Santa Anita. Imagine that—a column on thoroughbred horse racing in this most hi-brow of magazines. Eventually, it went the way of The Long-Winded Lady, Berton Roueche's Annals of Medicine, and the little quirks that characterized the magazine, such as the placement of the author's name at the end, rather than the beginning of a piece and the absence of a Table of Contents, all of which brought a little mystery to the reading experience. Should I peek at the author's name before I read the story? Should I thumb through the entire issue to learn what's in it? Who could have written this Talk of the Town piece, a question, like the first two, that is no longer necessary?

More than anything, I think the magazine communicated to me in those early days a standard of discourse and analysis that seemed to be worth emulating. It gave me a model to follow preparing the lectures for my classes and judging the work of others. I wanted to write as clearly and as thoughtfully and occasionally as humorously as the writers did on the pages of *The New Yorker,* and I expected others to do the same. I knew I had a long way to go, but *The New Yorker* pointed the way for me. In that respect, nothing has changed in the ensuing years.

In May of 2000, the magazine held a festival in New York to celebrate its 75th anniversary. Many of its well-known authors read from their work, some lectured, and others participated in panel discussions or gave interviews. The New Yorker Festival was such a success that it has been repeated every year since.

Think of it: the writers of a weekly magazine holding forth about their work during three full days of readings, lectures, and discussions. Outside academic society meetings, I can think of nothing else like it in this country, surely not by any other magazine or periodical. When I went to the Festival the following year, I was surprised by the large crowds at most of the events and the fact that, while most were from New York City, a goodly number had come from distant locations. I had traveled across the country from Oregon; one woman I met had come all the way from Honolulu.

What led me and so many others to travel so far, at some expense, to attend this Festival? More than anything, I think we came to make contact with a few of its talented contributors and to connect in some vague fashion with the community of readers and writers who recognize the unique and special value of the magazine. Many of its most notable contributors were present the year I attended.

On Fiction Night, which opened the Festival, I had to choose between Anne Beattie and Richard Ford, or Michael Cunningham and Deborah Eisenberg, or Nick Hornby and Zadie Smith, or Lorrie Moore and Julian Barnes, and other pairs no less notable. The choice was impossible. The seminars and presentations on each of the following two days were no less impressive.

David Remnick's interview of Woody Allen was far and away the most popular event of the Festival the year I attended. A huge room in the New York Public Library was used for the session. Woody ambled in and the crowd roared. Remnick, who seemed to be everywhere at the Festival, reported that the session sold out the day tickets went on sale. Woody admitted he was not a scholar, saying he is just Woody.

Everyone loved his modest, unassuming, and fun-loving self-deprecation. He was a natural at it and good at poking fun at much of modern life, without annoying anyone. He loves to write, hates leaving his apartment, and doesn't care what people say about his work; he just needs to do it. Otherwise, he would collapse. Woody offered an interesting view of greatness: you do what you do, you do what you do best, and if others like it or think it's great, then that's fine. And if they don't, that's fine too. But you always have to do what you like to do and what you do naturally. Talent is a gift, not something you can try to attain. You can work at perfecting it, but first it has to be there.

> With the exception of the recently introduced double issues, the magazine has been published every week for the past eighty-three years. Frankly, I find this rather astonishing. Putting together a magazine of this quality *week after week* for as many years as that (with no reason to believe it will be any different in the years ahead) seems something of a miracle to me.

> You have to stand before the bound volumes of the magazine on the shelves of any major library to really appreciate why I say this. When I found myself doing this the other day, I was dumbfounded by the row upon row of back issues of the magazine. Then, as I began my search for the Talk of the Town piece I wanted to cite, I realized I was going through one issue after another, as though it was the latest. Hours later, I found the piece I was seeking, although it would have taken but a moment had I had not been so caught up in thumbing through the old issues, page by page.

> Everything was still there. The advertisements for fashionable clothes and exotic places, the hilarious cartoons, the profiles of people-you-always-wanted-to-meet. The essays were longer then, but no less serious, and once they captured your interest, they took forever to finish. The same was true of the

Profiles, the Letters posted from European capitals or those unforgettable Pauline Kael film reviews, none of which seemed the least bit dated on rereading.

There were more short stories then and who would not want to re-read those that moved you the first time around; Cheever's "The Country Husband," Salinger's "A Perfect Day for Bananafish," William Maxwell's "What He Was Like", or Munro's, "The Jack Randa Hotel." Here still is classic literature about memorable people and situations that continue to bring pleasure and personal insights that you had not recognized before.

I can clearly recall the first time I read some of those stories and how I was affected by the experience. To cite an instance, I will never forget the first time I read "The Jack Randa Hotel," Munro's comedic tale of a fractured marriage and runaway husband. It was late in the afternoon, the day was warm, and I was in Italy, on the rooftop terrace of the hotel in Florence where I was staying. It was a *perfect moment*. I read her story slowly, very slowly, as I knew the moment would not last long or be repeated soon, if ever, again.

Like other longtime readers, I go through each issue, whether it's the print or digital edition, in a fairly regular fashion. I turn at once to the Table of Contents, also a recent addition, to learn who the writers are and on what subject they have written. Then I proceed, page by page, through the entire issue for the first time, reviewing the Talk of the Town, the cartoons, the poems, and the advertisements. After a suitable period of restraint, I commence reading a fair amount of each issue.

With few exceptions, I have been doing this every week for more than fifty years. Recently I have begun to wonder about the cumulative impact of this experience. How has this steady diet of reading *The New Yorker* influenced the life I lead or the work I do? Granted, this is a difficult question; I'm not sure it can ever be answered. Yet, in a way, isn't it the kind of question we might ask of any aesthetic or intellectual experience? How do the films we see, the books we read, or the theatrical events we attend influence us? These questions have always been difficult to answer.

But a lifelong experience of reading *The New Yorker* is not very different from those experiences and must surely leave an imprint upon its readers. Without any systematic research, there are two approaches one can take in trying to identify the nature of this influence. One can either imagine what a regular reader's life would be like without the magazine or, alternatively, recount in a concrete way how the magazine has shaped the actions they take and beliefs they hold. The first approach would yield a fairly speculative account; in fact, it would probably lead to several. So instead, I will adopt the second by considering my own experience, since *The New Yorker* continues to have a prominent place in my life.

As I begin to think about this matter, I realize that I read the magazine much the way I read most written materials. I make comments in the margins, copy notable passages, and duplicate articles that I want to save. An article has more than once motivated me to read more on a topic, undertake a research project, or turned my interests in a new direction. I often talk about the articles with friends and students. Some, like John Hersey's *Hiroshima* or Rachel Carson's *Silent Spring* and, more recently, Malcolm Gladwell's work on the *Tipping Point,* have spurred me to action and debate. I will often cite a *New Yorker* essay in the writing I do, and, from time to time, refer to them in the lectures I give.

In my social psychology class, to cite one instance, I often lecture about the effects of violence in the media. The students are always interested in the research on this issue, even if it is inconclusive. In preparing the lecture, I look over the material in my file each year to incorporate the latest studies and review those that I have found the most instructive. In doing so, I always re-read Pauline Kael's masterly review of "Bonnie and Clyde" that appeared in the October 21, 1967.

My first thought, of course, is that no one writes movie reviews with that kind of brilliance any more. But I don't speak about that with the students. Instead, I discuss her analysis of the role of violence in the film, and show how it anticipated future research findings on the impact of media violence. Kael wrote:

> *Such people [those who want to place legal restraints on movie violence] see "Bonnie and Clyde" as a danger to public morality; they think an audience goes to a play or a movie and takes the actions in it as examples for imitation. They look at the world and blame the movies. But if women who are angry with their husbands take it out on the kids, I don't think we can blame "Medea" for it; if, as has been said, we are a nation of mother-*

> *lovers, I don't think we can place the blame on "Oedipus Rex.*
>
> *The movies may set styles in dress or love-making, they may advertise cars or beverages, but art is not examples for imitation... people don't "buy" what they see in a movie quite so simply; Louis B. Mayer did not turn us into a nation of Andy Hardys, and if, in a film, we see a frightened man want only to take the life of another, it does not encourage us to do the same, any more than seeing an ivory hunter shoot an elephant makes us want to shoot one. It may, on the contrary, so sensitize us that we get a pang in the gut if we accidentally step on a moth.*

There is always a lively discussion after I read these passages, each of which makes an important point about the purported effects of exposure to film violence. This, in turns, gives me a chance to discuss current research on her claims. Kael's analysis brings our discussion of media violence into contact with the actual film-going experience of individuals who are thought to be influenced one way or another by violent films. This contrasts with the artificial nature of most laboratory studies in this area. Regrettably, because they support the views of those who wish to regulate the media, they are the ones most frequently cited in public policy discussions of this issue.

Every now and then, after mulling over a *New Yorker* piece, I will want to look further into a topic it has considered. That was certainly true in the case of Meghan Daum's article, "Virtual Love", that appeared in the August 25, 1997, issue, almost thirty years after Kael's review. Daum's essay, which the magazine placed in its "Brave New World Department", vividly recounts the reactions of a young woman to a romance that had originated on the Internet. It was not a happy experience, although when it began, Daum was instantly caught up in the "exhilaration" of digital courtship. She wrote:

> *But, curiously, the Internet felt anything but dehumanizing. My interaction with PFSlider seemed more authentic than much of what I experienced in the daylight realm of living beings. I was certainly putting more energy into the relationship than I had put into many others.*

Her essay led me to wonder about the features of electronic communication that might make it so essay to form online relationships, and whether these relationships differed from those established in the usual ways. I began by investigating the prevalence and durability of cyber-relationships. Daum reports that:

> *...at least seven people confessed to me the vagaries of their own E-mail affairs...This topic arose, unprompted, in the course of normal conversation. ...we all shook our heads in bewilderment as we told our tales...These were normal people, writers and lawyers and scientists. They were all smart, attractive, and more than a little sheepish about admitting just how deeply they had been sucked in. Mostly, it was the courtship ritual that had seduced us. E-*

> *mail had become an electronic epistle, a yearned-for rule book. It allowed us to do what was necessary to experience love.*

At the time, nothing was known about the frequency of cyber-romances. To find out, I surveyed over 1000 students with Internet accounts at a nearby university and was surprised to learn that 36% of those who responded indicated they had formed a close friendship with another individual in an online setting. 22% described it as a close romantic relationship. Even more surprising was the finding that, like Daum, the students did not characterize their on-line relationships as shallow or distant. Quite to the contrary, they claimed to have formed genuinely close friendships that were every bit as satisfying as those established in traditional ways. In fact, in some instances, they had led to marriage.

Most of the week I do research or devote myself to teaching. In either case, the subject matter almost always has something to do with psychology, primarily social or environmental. I am drawn by the relevance of these areas to everyday life. At times the research does capture my interest; occasionally it will even surprise me; but most of the time it does neither. Above all, it never fulfills a longing I seem to have for something of artistic or literary merit or something that emotionally gives me pause.

More often than not, *The New Yorker* comes to my rescue. There I find the culture that is absent from my ordinary world, and ideas that often seem truer than the ones I encounter in psychology. When I see the magazine in the mailbox, I must confess to being more than a little bit grateful that it has once again come my way. I welcome it like a close friend who stops by for a visit each week. *The New Yorker*, as former editor William Shawn put it, seems like "...an oasis...in a period in which so much of life is debased and corrupted." Yes, that is it precisely, even truer now than it was when he said it.

I know my *New Yorker* is not everyone's *New Yorker*. But in reading the magazine each week, I have come to feel part of the community of other readers who value polished writing and serious commentary. The symbolic nature of this community makes it no less real. In *The World Through a Monocle*, Mary Corey captured this bond quite well: "Some felt a profound kinship with the magazine because it spoke for them, giving a public voice to their own private intelligences." It says "what I think and feel," a Washington, D.C. woman wrote, "as I should like to have said it."

In a sense, *The New Yorker* has become my "Third Place"--a term coined by Ray Oldenberg to refer to those informal gathering places in the community that an individual is drawn to each day outside of their home and workplace. French cafes, English pubs and Italian piazzas are such places. I do not have a Third Place that I am drawn to at the end of the day.

However, at *The New Yorker,* I find a group of like-minded regulars who have come together for informal discussion and thoughtful banter and where someone can always be counted on for good story or an idea worth considering. I go in solitude and while I can't converse with them, later, in other settings, I can speak with others about the "discussion" that I have overheard at *The New Yorker*.

This is the kind of special relationship that is said to develop between *The New Yorker* and its readers, and the way in which the magazine has sustained and educated me during all the years that I have been a reader. One of the respondents to Ben Yagoda's survey of dedicated *New Yorker* readers recalled an experience she had while serving as a nurse during World War II in a remote section of northern Italy. She reported being asked by a wounded soldier, "If you could have anything right now, what would it be?" In an instant she replied, "An issue of *The New Yorker* magazine," whereupon the two--wounded soldier and American nurse, in that far off time and place--began reminiscing about their favorite *New Yorker* cartoons and writers. Deserted island, northern Italian hospital: I can't imagine responding any differently.

My Fictional Friends

Never, never did she feel in life the sense of recognition, the companionship, the great warm fact of solidarity that she found between the covers of a book.

Rachel Cusk
Arlington Park

In a strange way I have come to know and befriend some of the people in the books I read. They are usually individuals who confront the same problems I do, have the same aspirations and cultural sensitivities that I have or would like to have, if I was more sophisticated or better read. They are doing things I have done or dream about doing and they are doing them with greater depth and knowledge than I could ever hope to in my lifetime.

Moreover, I probably know some of my fictional friends better than my real ones. In *How to Read and Why* Harold Bloom wrote that one of the reasons we read *is* "Because you can know, intimately only a very few people, and perhaps you never know them at all. After reading The Magic Mountain you know Hans Castorp thoroughly, and he is greatly worth knowing."

Brian Morton's *Starting Out in the Evening* mesmerized me when I read it several years ago. The story concerns a young woman and a very old man, Leonard Schiller. Schiller is a writer. I have been trying to be one. His early novels had a profound influence on the woman, Heather Wolfe, a graduate student in literature. She arranges to meet him in order to gather materials for her thesis on his literary works. I have worked with attractive young women on their thesis. The novel describes the course of their relationship.

While that naturally charmed me, I was even more intrigued by the character of the old writer. He is 71, fat, fastidious and very slow afoot. He is not well, suffers from various ailments, although he hasn't lost his wit entirely. It was his age that got to me. I was not far removed from 71 when I read the book and was ill at the time, rather like Schiller. I dread being the way he was depicted in the tale--his slow shuffle, his ugly body, and lack of productivity. And I dreaded my illness that continued day after day, while I was reading about his.

Of course, all this contrasted with the youth, the spirit, and gumption of the young woman. This difference made the book for me. Not the witty, attractive Heather or the aging, infirm Schiller. Not the numerous philosophical insights scattered densely throughout the novel. But the striking contrast between youth and old age. Between a vigorous and talented young person and an old and weary man. For a moment, a very brief one, she made him feel young again. For a moment, she made me feel young again too.

Starting Out in the Evening was also chock-full of the sort of truths and philosophical insights that characterize serious fiction at its best. If literature can become a conversation between the reader and the character on the page, this book, at least in my case, was an exemplar.

M: *If life had taught her anything—if she had a philosophy of life—it probably boiled down to that: Go with the skid.*

K: Perhaps so. At times I wish I had been able to able to go with the skid. Things might have been a bit different. But then it wouldn't have been me.

M: *Life made more sense in the Middle Ages, when no one lasted past forty.*

K: I often think how how much truth there is to this idea. What is the purpose of going on day after day without anything to show for it, other than a co-payment receipt from the doctor?

M: *...brain-dead aura of the suburbs.*

K: Love that phrase. It captures my experience in the suburbs exactly. It is all encompassing and associated with great wave of sleepiness.

Morton's novel was a sad tale of an aging and infirm author, whose writing life was over but who could still be moved by another person. As I read the book, I saw all too much of myself in Schiller. But I also enjoyed being surprised by his insights and chatting about them with him. We don't have an easy time knowing ourselves. Sometimes a good book makes our task a little easier, to say nothing of the pleasure it gives to talk things over with someone else.

Do the fictional friendships we have bespeak of some kind of malady? Other perfectly normal readers seem to have the same kind of relationships. In *So Many Books, So Little Time*, Sara Nelson writes: *"I talk about my books as if they were people, and I choose them the way I choose my friends; because somebody nice introduced us, because I like their looks, because the best of them turn out to be smart and funny and both surprising and inevitable at the same time."*

In her introduction to Alice Munro's short story, *The Bear Came Over the Mountain Sarah*, Sarah Polley commented that *"...I have had a relationship with this story that has been a powerful and as transformative as any I have had with another human being."*

Polley's expression is surely one most powerful and moving statements I have read about the effects of reading literature. She notes that *"The Bear Came Over the Mountain entered my life when I was twenty-one years old. It crept right into me, had its way with me, and shifted my direction in ways I didn't understand until years later."*

She was inspired by Munro's story to adapt and direct a film version, *Away From Her*. Julie Christie stars as a woman suffering the early stages of Alzheimer's that progresses further and further into darkness. Her husband of 44 years struggles not to lose her while she, in turn, drifts away. Polley says the story reshaped her idea of love and led her to a place that *"I am very, very grateful to be."*

James Schall in *The Unseriousness of Human Affairs* writes, *"The reader will find many of my friends in this book, both friends that I know and...many whom I have never met, yet know through reading, through having been taught about them and by them."* But what types of friends are they? Some live with us forever, while others drift away soon after the story concludes. But did you ever hear of someone falling in love with a literary friend?

Elizabeth Hawes in her book, *Camus, a Romance*, says, *"During my last college years, I had photograph of Albert Camus prominently displayed above my desk...I had fallen in love with him. Not romantic love in the only sense I had experienced in those days...but something deeper, like the bonding of two souls."*

She says Camus had an enormous impact on her life, that his insights literally changed its course. *"I had never before experienced such an intimate relationship with a writer, poring over his prose and filling up with his rhythms, thinking his thoughts, trying to crawl under his skin."*

Her feelings led Hawes on a lifelong search to learn more about this very private man. *Camus, a Romance* is a fascinating portrait of Camus, the man and the writer. It chronicles her experiences following in his footsteps in North Africa, Paris, New York and Provence. In an effort to come to some kind of understanding of this complex man, she tracked down his friends, members of his family, and the writers that knew him

Her journey reminded me of a comparable one by the classical language teacher, Raimund Gregorious.

However, Gregorious was not a writer, rather he was one of the central characters in Pascal Mercier's masterful novel, *Night Train to Lisbon*. Gregorious had been teaching at the same secondary school in Berne Switzerland for decades. He was fixed in the same, daily solitary routine and had no desire to change it.

> *Mundus, the most reliable and predictable person in this building and probably the whole history of the school, working here for more than thirty years, impeccable in his profession...respected and even feared in the university for his astounding knowledge of ancient languages...his head also held the Hebrew that had amazed several Old Testament scholars.*

On his way to school one day he encounters a distraught woman on a bridge who says her mother tongue is Portuguese. The woman walks with Gregorious to his class, sits there for a while, then departs. Soon thereafter Gregorious realizes his own life is drawing to a close and suddenly walks out of the classroom to the utter astonishment of his students.

> *...Simply to get up and go: what courage! He just got up and went, the students keep saying. Just got up and went.*

He eventually winds up in Spanish language bookstore where he chances upon an antique Portuguese book, *A Goldsmith of Words* by Amadeu de Prado. He buys the book and a Portuguese dictionary, begins reading, is astonished by the power and the beauty of the words and the next morning leaves Switzerland, his school, and his daily routine to take the train to Portugal on a journey to track down the life and world of Amadeu de Prado.

> *...he had the amazing feeling, both upsetting and liberating, that at the age of fifty-seven, he was about to take his life into his own hands for the first time.*

Like Hawes's relationship with Camus, the one I had with the characters in *Night Train to Lisbon* was a strong as any I have had in reading literary fiction. I entered into the lives of Raimund Gregorious and Amadeu de Prado. I admired them, thought about the same questions they posed on every page, and found myself just as perplexed by them as they did. And I came to know these fictional characters as well as any of the friends I have in real life, actually in some respects even better. This is the kind of encounter that can sometimes link a book with a reader and make the experience of reading literature so compelling.

You form your friendships where you find them. They can be anyone, anywhere, at anytime. In *Companionable Books*, George Gordon writes,

> *What most men and women are looking for all their lives is companionship...There is a companionable quality in some books that skips the centuries...*

The neurosurgeon, Henry Perowne, in Ian McEwan's *Saturday* is as real to me as anyone I will ever hope to meet. I continue to think about his ideas, his medical expertise and his sense of humor. Perowne's daughter is a poet and he is amused by her tutorials to try to get him up to speed about literature.

In turn, I was entertained by their delightful banter and the ironic exchanges they have about his disinterest in following her lead. And it is clear that Perowne isn't much of a reader. No, Henry is a scientist devoted to his work and the promise he sees in neurophysiology. Still he is restless, at times silently dissatisfied with his life, and yearns for something more. If it is anything, the missing element is music.

> *There's nothing in his own life that contains this inventiveness, this style of being free. The music speaks to unexpressed longing or frustration, a sense that he's being denied himself an open road, the life of the heart celebrated in the songs. There has to be more to life than merely saving lives.*

It's hard to find a friend quite like Henry Perowne. But he became a close friend during the time I was reading the book. I greatly enjoyed his company and the chance to spend some time with him.

And once in a while, I think back on our conversations and return to the ideas we discussed. It seems we had a good deal in common especially our tendency to spend part of each day ruminating about one thing or another and examining the contents of our mind down to the smallest synapse.

After I finished Elliot Perlman's *Seven Types of Ambiguity,* I was entertained by what the reviewers had to say about it. One described it as "fat, pretentious" an "embarrassment" and could not believe it was ever published. Another noted

Perlman's "talent for sharp satire," and said that portions of the book were "marvelous stuff." Still another vacillated between "distinctly odd" and an "exciting gamble of a novel." Isn't this bizarre? What can a reader make of these differences? Shall I read the book or not? There is only one way. Forget about the critics and give the book a try. I did and I found it immensely rewarding.

I also noticed the way the reviewers were silent about the effects this ambitious novel had on them personally. Instead they went about evaluating the text or Perlman's writing skill or lack thereof. I suppose that is the customary practice. Critics don't talk much about how a book affects them personally

For example, the critics didn't tell you how they *felt* about 32-year-old Simon Heywood, the central figure who is depicted from seven different perspectives, including his own. What did they think about Simon? What kind of experience did they have in reading about him? Did his life and dilemmas reflect anything about their own life or contemporary life in general?

Yes, I found Simon an altogether likeable person whose plight I understood quite well, as it was in some respects similar to my own. Perlman writes: *"...readers usually identify with one or other of the characters in a story...That is why most of them read fiction in the first place."* In one way or another this is true of most of my fictional friends.

It isn't at all odd that I identified with Simon. While I did not loose my teaching position because of budgetary cutbacks or because of any impropriety, true or not, I did leave the academic world long before my time had come. And while I do not drink or live a lethargic life with a prostitute, even one as beautiful as Angelique, my life is drifting aimlessly now in much the same way his did.

Simon also never fit in, he never found a world that accepted his quirky views or made the most of his versatile mind. He says:

> *I was just not cut out for the business of living at a time like this, a time when wondering, caring, dreaming…they were just not selling, they were uncool, unhip, not sexy.*

That mirrored my sense of him perfectly. Simon read poetry at a time when not many others did. He really had no one to talk with about the poems, the music, the movies, the history and the politics that were important to him. Not even Anna, the Anna who had rejected him in spite of or perhaps because of his deep love for her. She says, *" I wasn't any longer feeling augmented by him but diminished."* I doubt I would have felt so diminished. Instead, I know I would have enjoyed talking with Simon about the arts, culture, and ideas that he was drawn to.

I too have never felt truly comfortable in any of the places I've lived or worked. None of my views ever really met with much favor other than to a few kindly students and an occasional friend. I have always felt just as much alone in this respect as Simon. Like him, I too became somewhat of a recluse, dislocated from much of the world around me, opted out of an ordinary life.

At times I thought about moving to Europe, to a country where culture, mostly the reading tradition, seems to be more highly valued than it is in America. But I knew whatever it was that I hoped to achieve by doing that could, with a little searching, be found right here, in my own neighborhood, if I really wanted to make the effort. It was just another of my adolescent longings.

But then Simon did something stupid. He "abducted" or so it was claimed, Anna's son, who he had previously unbeknownst to Anna and her husband, saved from drowning in their pool. Here, of course, my life departed from his, but not my sympathy for what Simon had to deal with after this act. You help a friend in need. I would have liked to have helped Simon get through the consequences of what he admits was an irrational and futile act.

I enjoyed reading about how much Simon loved teaching, how he seemed early on to thrive in the experience of teaching young children. Of course, I too loved teaching in the beginning. It is why I came to a college where teaching was central to the academic enterprise. The students continued to make it worthwhile, at least they did for many years. I would have enjoyed comparing notes with Simon about our days in the classroom.

To my way of thinking Simon was a very bright, beguiling young man, full of ideas, many of them seemingly crazy but on analysis ever so sensible who was thoroughly misunderstood by just about everyone, even his therapist who often seemed utterly befuddled by what Simon did and thought. I never thought Simon was depressed as others did, at least, in its clinical form. Rather I thought he was simply a little melancholic, not without justification in my view, and he was unhappy, sometimes very much so, just like everyone else. As Alex, his therapist notes: *"Simon has always been, other than for short periods, too involved in things to be clinically depressed."*

There wasn't any pretense to Simon; he was totally honest and up front about everything. That surely doomed him to anything approaching a normal life. Simon also knew as well as anybody else who he was. In describing himself, he says:

> *I was a man of more than average intelligence seasoned by years of wide and considered reading, a man of not unpleasing visage and of some awareness of the mighty winds and faint breezes that move the world, a man sensitive both to the plight of the many and to that of the man in his shirt sleeves ambling through the leaves in the city park during his lunch hour, desperately trying to keep his own tepid inconsequence at bay with every short and timid breath.*

He knew his best and he knew his worst, knew how perfectly rational he could be at one time and then at another fall into a web of destructive obsession. Aren't we all a mixture of two or more selves? And so it was not difficult to admire Simon, to want to read every one of the six hundred odd pages of *Seven Types of Ambiguity* to learn how things worked out for him. For a very long time Simon was a literary friend of mine and at times a shadowy reflection of myself, as well.

I have quite a few fictional friends, probably more than are alive and about the only ones I have now. They offer me the pleasure of their company. They engage me in conversation, pose questions, pass along ideas worthy of consideration, and point the way out of the minor dilemmas that unsettle my days.

It is a treat to know them. They don't shout or insult me and from time to time they are a source of those truths that do not, as so many have said before, appear in any source other than literature. Who could ask for more of any friend, fictional or otherwise? Proust is said to have compared our real friends to those we meet on the page, because both types of friendships involve communion with others. He also noted that those you chance upon in reading have a key advantage:

> *In reading, friendship is suddenly brought back to its original purity. There is no false amiability with books. If we spend the evening with these friends, it is because we genuinely want to.*

An Inquiring Mind

Gregorius did what he had always done when he was unsure: He opened up a book.

Pascal Mercier

What can we learn about an individual from the books they write or the accounts of their friends, family members or lovers? I am confronted by this question as I try to tell you about two individuals-- Amadeu de Prado and Raimund Gregorious and why I admired them so much. I never met either of these men, nor did anyone else as far as I can tell. Rather they are the fictional creations of a Swiss novelist and philosopher writing under the name of Pascal Mercier in his novel, *Night Train to Lisbon*. This makes the task of drawing a portrait of Prado and Gregorious even more difficult, also more fun.

There is really very little plot to the novel. Indeed, one reviewer noted it is largely talk—talk, talk, talk. That is true but even more it is mostly questions—questions, questions, questions. That is precisely why I liked the novel so much and why I liked the individuals who raised all these questions in the first place.

The questions posed issues I have given a good deal of thought to and have been thinking about a good deal of my life or they posed new ones that I felt deserved to be considered. It is a rare treat to read a novel about such individuals and an even greater one to carry on a conversation with them as I sometimes do when I talk to the fictional characters in the books I read.

Night Train to Lisbon begins by describing a typical day in the life of Raimund Gregorious, a day that is as fixed and orderly as any other day in his life—at least in the beginning. Gregorious, is a classics professor and linguistic scholar living in Bern, Switzerland with proficiency in at least a half dozen languages and a vast knowledge of ancient history and texts.
Following a bizarre series of events on what otherwise would have been his daily walk to the school where he teaches, Gregorious comes in possession of volume written by a Portuguese physician, Amadeu de Prado. He is overtaken by the volume's eloquence and intellectual brilliance and is so consumed by its contents that in striking departure from his daily routine, he leaves his class in mid-session and sets off for Portugal to learn more about the author and the sources of his extraordinary document.

He learns that the author was a highly respected doctor, a brilliant scholar and a member of the resistance movement in opposition to the Portuguese dictator Antonio Salazar.

Gregorious asks: *"Was it possible that the best way to make sure of yourself was to know and understand someone else?"* Perhaps because of his growing sense that his time was running out, as well as his curiosity about Prado, Gregorious comes to realize that he would like to know everything he can about him. This quest brings him into contact with Prado's two sisters, a close friend, and two women, the "untouched" loves of his life.

While Gregorious's spur-of-the-moment breakout quest to Lisbon and encounters with these individuals is not without its appeal, it was not the major reason I found *Night Train to Lisbon* every bit as fascinating as Gregorious found the Portuguese volume. Rather it was the questions Amadeu de Prado raised in his volume, *A Goldsmith of Words*, and in turn considered by Gregorious as he read the text and brooded over its rich and varied meanings. As is my practice, I recorded the passages in the novel that struck me as noteworthy for one reason or another. And when I reviewed those I had collected, I realized how many were framed as questions, often one after another in cascade of queries.

Consider the following examples concerned with one of the central issues of the novel—how one comes to know another person, including oneself.

> *The stories others tell about you and the stories you tell about yourself: which come closer to the truth?*
>
> *In such stories, is there really a difference between true and false?*
>
> *What do we know of somebody if we know nothing of the images passed to him by his imagination?*
>
> *To understand yourself: Is that a discovery or a creation?*

What difficult questions. Who has not wondered about them at one time or another? How complicated and unknowable we are. How then can we ever expect to know another person? Mercier writes:

> *We are in the dark about so many of our wishes and thoughts, and others sometimes know more about them than we do.*

And, as if to take issue with current empirical research on person perception, he proclaims: *Inside a person it is much more complicated than our schematic, ridiculous explanations wanted to have us believe.*

In a similar vein, Mercier by way of Prado wonders a great deal about the problem of identity. Who are we anyway? Are we the same person today that we were 40 years ago? If so, what is it that constitutes our core or does that concept mean anything at all? Prado inquires:

> *When was somebody himself? When he was as always? As he saw himself? Or as he was when the white hot lava of thoughts and feelings buried all lies, masks, and self-deceptions?*

> *Is there a mystery under the surfaces of human action? Or are human beings utterly what their obvious acts indicate?*

Does it make any sense to say that a person has a central self, a distinctive identity that lies hidden behind most of the actions that constitute daily life? I sometimes find myself in the presence of another person who for entirely unknown reasons calls forth expressions that somehow seem far more myself than is usually the case. How does that happen? Who is the me that appears in such situations and how does it differ from my other self or selves? Nothing that I have been able to detect in the other person seems responsible. But what I am on those rare occasions is instantaneous and continuous and thoroughly exhilarating. It seems entirely natural and I have no idea what to make of it.

Gregorious had devoted his life to a linguistic scholarship, so he was naturally drawn to Prado's frequent speculations about language and his amazement, *"That words could cause something in the world, make someone move or stop, laugh or cry..."* Elsewhere he asks:

> *Saying something to another: how can we expect it to affect anything?*
>
> *How could a person almost lose his mind because a word, a single word, that occurred one single time, had escaped him?*

These questions always remain unanswered. Neither Prado or Gregorious considered how one might go about trying to examine them or what others have said about these issues. The questions just keep unfolding, one after the other, each one as interesting as the one before. Many are the subjects of current research and writing in the cognitive sciences, the discussion of which is surely out of place in the novel, but on the mind of anyone vaguely familiar with this field. The extraordinary popularity of Malcolm Gladwell's recent book, *Blink: The Power of Thinking without Thinking* is a case in point, as it takes up the very same issue Prado poses in his question about the relative merits of analytical and intuitive decision-making. The same is true for other recent works on the extent to which irrational, non-conscious processes govern far more of the decision making process than we usually believe.

Throughout his volume, Prado reflects on the sources of human thought and action. He knows how difficult it is to identify them with any precision, that they vary widely between individuals, and from one day to the next.

> *If it is the enchanting light of a shimmering August day that produces clear, sharp-edged shadows, the thought of a hidden human depth seems bizarre and like a curious, even slightly touching fantasy.... On the other hand, if city and river are clouded over on a dreary January day by a dome of shadowless light and boring gray, I know no greater certainty than this: that all human action is only an extremely imperfect, ridiculously helpless expression of a hidden internal life of unimagined depths that presses to the surface without ever being able to reach it even remotely.*

At the time he wrote *A Goldsmith of Words* Portugal was under the sway of the dictator, Alberto Salazar. After saving the life of the head of Salazar's secret police under conditions that depended more on his obligations as a physician than political allegiance, Prado joined the resistance. At this point his life became even more perilous than it was for any intellectual at that time. The subject of violent behavior, especially interpersonal violence is a constant theme of his volume.

> *What could it mean to deal appropriately with anger?*
>
> *What can it mean to train ourselves in anger and imagine that we take advantage of its knowledge without being addicted to its poison?*
>
> *Why did our parents, teachers and other instructors never talk to us about it? Why didn't they tell something of this enormous significance? Not give us in this case any compass that could have helped us avoid wasting our soul on useless, self-destructive anger?*

For all his brilliance, enthusiasms, and honesty, Prado was a melancholy man who in most respects stood apart from others. He felt his isolation keenly, writing:

> *Encounters between people, it often seems to me, are like crossings of racing trains at breakneck speed in the deepest night. We cast fleeting, rushed looks at the others sitting behind dull glass in dim light, who disappear from our field of visions as soon as we barely have time to perceive them.*

And he kept searching for someone who understood him, who could keep up with him, who was as alive and questioning as he was. He asked:

> *And why had he never had a friend as Jorge O'Kelly had been for Prado--A friend with whom he could have talked about things like loyalty and love, and about death?*

> *What is it that we call loneliness, it can't simply be the absence of others, you can be alone and not lonely, and you can be among people and yet be lonely? So what is it?*

> *Is it so that everything we do is done out of fear of loneliness? ...Why else do we hold on to all these broken marriages, false friendships, boring birthday parties? What would happen if we refused all that, put an end to the skulking blackmail and stood on our own?*

In reading *Night Train to Lisbon* I was not deliberately looking for passages that posed questions. It was only after finishing the book and began to look closely at those I had recorded that I realized how many were framed this way. In fact, of the 120 passages I recorded from the book, a number that may be the most in my reading history included at least one question 47 (40%). I began to wonder if questioning also played a similar role in the passages I recorded from other books that have meant a lot to me.

I copied 46 passages from Ian McEwan's *Saturday*, a book I enjoyed every bit as much as *Night Train to Lisbon* but of these quotations, only 7 (15%) included a question. Similarly, I recorded 47 passages in Philip Roth's *Exist Ghost* and of these only 7 (15%) included a question. And of the 83 passages I recorded in Eliot Perlman's *Seven Types of Ambiguity*, just 7 (8%) included a question. In contrast, I recorded 83 passages in Rachel Cusk's *Arlington Park*, a book that entranced me for days, and of these 28 (41%)

included a question, a value that is approximately the same as Mercier's tale.

It is clear from this small sample that questioning is not a critical feature of the novels I like most. I may enjoy that style of writing and tend to think that way myself, but it probably plays little if any role in my reading preferences. Henry Perowne, the central character in Ian McEwan's *Saturday* is depicted as a deeply reflective man who spends a good part of that day at least, wondering about a wide range of topics. But his reflections are rarely formulated as questions.

It would be interesting to compare writers on this dimension. Do some employ questioning more than others and if so, what might be responsible for their practice? Do they come from a particular tradition or are they, like Pascal Mercier, from his discipline (philosophy) where questioning is a central practice? Regardless, it reflects a style of writing that is one of probing and wrestling with ideas. Many of Prado's questions are posed for rhetorical effect rather than a direct answer. Prado says: *We humans: what do we know of one another?* Clearly he implies that we know very little. Still he wants the reader to consider the issue and give some thought to the implied answer. It is a style of writing that encourages an internal dialogue for any reader who takes the text seriously.

In addition to a style of writing, I have noticed a similar manner in the way individuals converse with one another. Some ask a great many questions, while others might ask one or two and, more commonly, none at all. Perhaps questioning as a mode of conversation, indeed, as a way of thinking, is a distinct personality dimension. My hunch is that it is strongly associated with a philosophical turn of mind, a general skepticism about most beliefs, at least, a continuing effort to look more deeply into the claims of others whether they are expressed in conversation or the printed page. That is clearly true of Amadeu and Gregorious.

In contrast, other individuals seem more accepting of whatever it is they hear or read and tend to comment, if they say anything at all, with a "That is really interesting" or "It reminds me of this or that" or simply change the subject altogether. They are unlikely to express any doubts or seek clarification or evidence, especially contrary evidence, relevant to the matter at hand.

Those of the questioning frame of mind use an approach not unlike that of a Socratic dialogue where conversation becomes a progression of questions designed to arrive at a conclusion beyond the originally stated position. Some people are quite comfortable with this kind of discussion. For them it becomes a truly joint exchange in the interest of clarifying thinking and sharpening beliefs and perhaps even learning something along the way. I sense those of the accepting frame of mind do not fall naturally into this mode of conversation and perhaps might find it difficult to sustain for very long.

And so it went from one page to the next, from one set of questions to the next. A remarkable journey that began by abandoning an orderly life dedicated to classical languages for one in pursuit of an author he had never heard of, who had written a book in an unknown language, and lived in a city that he had never been to. He begins to translate the book, is captivated by its introspective musings, and one by one encounters the individuals Amadeu de Prado wrote about in *A Goldsmith of Words*. The tale is beautifully written and the questions it poses linger long in my mind, as does the reflective mood of the tale and its central characters.

In a word, some of my favorite novels have few if any questions, while others have a great many. They set me off in another direction for a moment, my mind wanders off the page, I elaborate the tale or move it to another place. I don't rewrite the story, but may embellish it a bit. I read more actively as I grapple with the questions or make all the associations that come with experience and a lifetime of study. In a way, I reply to the author who, with his questions, invites me to join with him telling the story. It is a reading experience at its best.

On Literary Truth

> *I think a great book--leaving aside other qualities such as narrative power, characterization, style and so on--is a book that describes the world in a way that has not been done before; and that is recognized by those who read it as telling new truths--about society or the way in which emotional lives are led, or both--such truths having not been previously available, certainly not from official records or government documents, or from journalism or television.*
>
> Julian Barnes

I would be less inclined to read fiction were it not for the truths I find there. These are truths that, as others have said, one rarely finds elsewhere. In commenting on volume one of her autobiography, Doris Lessing concluded that...*fiction is better at the truth than a factual record. Why this should be so is a very large subject and one I don't begin to understand.*

In trying to unravel Lessing's puzzlement about the nature of literary truths, I have looked more closely at those I have collected in my Commonplace Book. For the most they seem to fall into one of four general categories: Conceptual Truths, Personal Truths, Hypothetical Truths, and Aesthetic Truths.

Conceptual Truth: A passage that reinforces a belief, value or moral conviction that I hold, often one that is not widely held and so its literary expression makes it especially noteworthy.

There are a great many passages of this kind in Zia Haider Rahman's *In the Light of What We Know*. Ideas abound throughout the novel. For example, a discussion of mathematics occurs early in the first chapter, the beauty and satisfaction it brings to Zafar, the novel's central character.

Godel's Incompleteness Theorem is introduced:

> *Within any given system, there are claims which are true but which cannot be proven to be true.*
>
> *Described as the greatest mathematical discovery of the last century, it is a theorem with the simple message that the farthest reaches of what we can ever know fall short of the limits of what is true, even in mathematics.*

Memory is a frequent topic throughout the novel as Zafar attempts to recount the irregular path of his experiences while reflecting on the limits and quirks of memory. He says, for example, *"Our memories do not visit us in chronology, and the story we form by joining up the memories involves choices with the purpose of making a whole and finding a pattern."*

Later he notes, *"This conversation took place last year. If I were to put my finger on what it is about it that makes it significant in my mind, I would have to declare that I don't readily know."*

Personal Truth: A passage that reveals something about myself (or one that I had not recognized before), as well as a correspondence between some aspect of my life and that of a character in a story.

Colm Toibin writes in *The Master*:

> *Everyone he knew carried with them the aura of another life which was half-secret and half-open, to be known about but not mentioned.....He remembered the shock when he first came to know Paris, the culture of easy duplicity, the sense he got of these men and women, watched over by the novelists, casually withholding what mattered to them most.*

I also recorded twelve separate descriptions of what I call the two-selves experience. My favorite is drawn from a famous Chekov's short story, sometimes translated, *The Lady with the Toy Dog,*

> *He had two lives; one obvious, which every one could see and know, if they were sufficiently interested, a life full of conventional truth and conventional fraud, exactly like the lives of his friends and acquaintances; and another, which moved underground. And by a strange conspiracy of circumstances, everything that was to him important, interesting, vital, everything than enabled him to be sincere and denied self-deception and was the very core of his being, must dwell hidden away from others, and everything that made him false, a mere shape in which he hid himself in order to*

> *conceal the truth, as for instance his work in the bank, arguments at the club, his favorite gibe about women, going to parties with his wife---all this was open.*

Hypothetical Truth: The passages in this group pose a question or put forward a hypothesis that seems original or usual in some respect, one that warrants inquiry or confirms a finding that I have read about before.

In *The Black Violin* Maxence Fermine writes, *There is nothing worse than having been truly happy once in your life. From that moment on, everything makes you sad, even the most insignificant things.*

Similarly, in *Apprentice to the Flower Poet* Debra Weinstein suggests, *As civilization advances, poetry declines.*

And Joseph Epstein writes in *Fabulous Small Jews*, *...essentially you could not persuade anyone to give up something that gave him intense pleasure.*

Aesthetic Truth: A passage that has captured my attention or is so well written that it has a certain quality that one can only call beautiful. Its truth consists in being true to real life or, as Seilmann & Larsen have pointed out, has the character of verisimilitude. Here is an example by Andre Aciman from *Pensione Eolo*,

> *That winter, when it was all over, I would walk or ride a bus past her building. Sometimes I'd think how lucky I'd been to have spent a year with her there and how*

> *gladly I would give everything I now had to be back with the same woman, staring out those windows whenever she went sulking into the other room, imagining and envying those strolling outside, never once suspecting that one day soon I might be a stroller, too, looking in envying the man I'd been there once, knowing all along, though that if I had to do it over again, I'd still end where I was, yearning for those days when I was living with a woman I had never loved and would never love but in whose home I had...invented a woman who, like me was neither here nor there.*

The truths conveyed by these passages may also be uniquely true for me. That is the wonderful thing about literature: it makes no claims of universality, it is not true or false in the way an empirical proposition is. Rather we read ourselves *into* literature without concern, as we are in science, for whether or not the passage is true for others, and if so, for how many and to what degree.

Phyllis Rose expresses a similar view in her recent book on Marcel Proust.

> *...but what I looked forward to most in reading Proust were revelations about myself.....Proust understood that every reader, in reading, reads himself. Far from minding this, he saw it as the writer's task to facilitate it. Thus the writer's word is merely a kind of optical instrument which he offers to the reader to enable him to discern what, without this book he would perhaps*

> *never have perceived in himself. And the recognition by the reader in his own self of what the book says is proof of its veracity.*

Here Rose suggests that the power of literature lies in confirming those truths about our self that we rarely encounter in our daily experience. In a certain respect, then, reading is not unlike the practice of science. In doing science we seek to test our ideas and when they are confirmed, we experience some degree of satisfaction. Similarly, it is no less of a satisfaction when in reading a work of literature we see our self reflected on the page or a confirmation that helps us to make sense of the world in which we live.

Are these two cultures really incompatible? Cannot one hold simultaneously to the different forms of truth, to the general truths of science and the specific truths of literature? In writing to me about this topic Audrey Borenstein quotes the following passage from her book *Redeeming the Sin: Social Science and Literature*:

> *The social scientist, too, needs experience, observation, and imagination; and the best of social science, the works that will endure, are those in which all three are interwoven. Yet, while the risk for the social scientist is that he may miss seeing the detail— the trees, the risk of the writer is that he may miss seeing the forest. It would seem that the social scientist and the writer work from different directions toward the same achievement, the*

> *discovery of the universal. Ultimately, however, the distinction between artistic and scientific endeavor is arbitrary and spurious...The crystal and the molecule, the spinning earth, the leaf moving in the wind are rightful subjects for both poet and naturalist: artist and scientist are not two beings, but one.*

I have also come to believe that it isn't necessary to choose between these two cultures, that they go hand in hand, much like so many other so-called dualities that are said to characterize contemporary life, say, for example, between solitude and socializing, between marriage and autonomy, between the public and private self.

There may be little disagreement about this once it is recognized that literary and empirical accounts have entirely different goals. In a recent interview Daniel Gilbert, an experimental social psychologist, comments that *"most of what science has to tell us about human behavior already has been divined by writers with great insight."* In response to a later question Gilbert admits that there's nothing about *"human behavior or the experience of the mind that you cannot find in literature. But on the other hand you can also find the opposite in literature. Everything that can be said about the human condition has been said by some writer."*

He notes that after reading his most recent book, *Stumbling on Happiness* where he liberally quotes Shakespeare, a literature professor said, *"Given that*

Shakespeare saw all this stuff, had these insights, why do we need science?" He answers, *"Well I could also find ten places where he said exactly the opposite. If you say everything, some of it winds up being right."*

But even science, at least the science of human behavior, is stuck with considerable empirical uncertainty. Facts and theories come and go with further research; what is held to be true today will in due course shown to be false or incomplete or require revision tomorrow. As Gilbert later admits, he always begins his freshman course, Introduction to Psychology, by telling the students *"that half of what I teach them will turn out to be wrong; the problem is I don't know which half.*

This is precisely what he said about Shakespeare. Indeed, in the psychological sciences the level of inconsistency and disagreement between accounts is scarcely distinguishable from literary accounts. A literary truth is always right, right for its fictional depiction, and right for those readers who finds it expresses something true for them. It may not be true for other readers. But a writer has no designs on formulating general truths, as he does if he is doing science.

In a discussion of his literary education Joseph Epstein discusses why he was drawn to literature and the literary life he now leads. In writing about the work of social scientists Epstein says, *Scientists and social scientists claim to operate by induction, but there are grounds for thinking that they do not, not really; that instead they are testing hopefully, hunches, which they call hypotheses. But novelists and poets, if they are true to their craft, are not out to prove anything.*

And later: *"One of the most important functions of literature in the current day is to cultivate a healthy distrust of the ideas thrown up by journalism and social science."* This leaves open the question how and in what ways literature gives rise to this skepticism. For it was something I learned very early on in my own studies of social science, particularly from its methodology and mode of analysis.

In speaking of the truths to be found in literature Epstein also writes that *James [Henry] felt that there were truths above the level of ideas, truths of the instincts, of the heart, of the soul, and these were truths that James, once he had attained to his literary mastery, attempted to plumb in his novels and stories.*

Many other writers have reflected on the nature of literary truth. I find what they have to say a refreshing antidote to everything I had learned about scientific truth, particularly the truths revealed by the discipline of experimental psychology. The passages below are among those that I have collected on the subject.

> *...we never get closer to the truth than in a novel.* Louis Begley

> *The reason why we like a book is because we say, Yes, because life is like that, and the reason why we stop reading certain kinds of childish books is because we say, Good story but life's not like that. The whole question of recognition is terribly important and that's why as you get older your reading experience inevitably gets richer because you have more of your own experience to bring to it."* Tim Parks

He liked novels because they dealt with the incommensurable in life, with the things that couldn't be expressed another way. Richard Ford

Psychologists seek to establish very general laws of human thought and action. However, I never understood how evidence derived by averaging the scores of a group of individuals could serve as the foundation for a science of *individual* behavior. Laws based on such aggregate data tell us very little about specific individuals and serve only to obscure crucial features of human variability and uniqueness. Literature points the spotlight on them.

Further, the many exceptions to those general laws severely limit their generality. Thus, it is impossible to say with much confidence that they hold for an individual at a particular time and place. I have come to believe that psychology will always have to be content with this sort of limitation. Laws based on aggregate data hold for some people, some of the time, but one never can be sure on any given occasion, if they apply to an individual in the situation at hand.

In contrast, literary truths hold for particular individuals and situations. They make no claims beyond that. They do not require testing or verification or large sample statistical analysis. Their veracity cannot be doubted, they are without exception true for the individual or situation at that time and place, and they are bound to be different for each person and situation.

Philosophical Novels

What is a philosophical novel? On my understanding, it is work of fiction that treats the same ideas and questions that philosophers have considered for centuries--moral, existential, and metaphysical. It is a novel where you ponder these issues, pause to consider them, make a note in the margin, or discuss with another individual. And you do all these things and more with a really notable novel of ideas.

In the *Wall Street Journal* (3/6/10) Rebecca Goldstein mentions five examples that she admires—*Herzog, Middlemarch, The Holy Sinner, The Black Prince* and *Einstein's Dreams*. How are these philosophical novels distinguished from those that are not?

In writing about Iris Murdoch's *The Black Prince*, Goldstein says, *"Like all the novels of ideas I admire, this one hides its high purpose under well-developed characters and an organic plot."* She notes that Mann's *The Holy Sinner "buries its seriousness beneath the seductions of story telling.'*

She says *Herzog* blends *"high-mindedness and low farce"* and that George Eliot's *Middlemarch* is *"imprinted with many of Spinoza's ideas."* Finally, she notes that *Einstein's Dreams* concerns the nature of time *"The play of ideas is heady as Alan Lightman wrests irony, pathos and poetry out of the abstractions of physics..."*

Goldstein's characterization of Lightman's novel comes closest to my conception of a philosophical novel. Yet she never frames her discussion of this novel or any of the four others in terms of how the reader might respond to the ideas or questions in the various ways I've indicated. Time. What is time? The abstractions of physics. What are they and is there any hope that I can understand them? Where can I learn more out about them?

In an interview in the *Paris Review* (#192) Ray Bradbury expresses a rather unusual view. *"Science fiction is the fiction of ideas... Science fiction is any idea that occurs in the head and doesn't exist yet, but soon will, and will change everything for everybody, and nothing will ever be the same again. As soon as you have an idea that changes some small part of the world you are writing science fiction. It is always the art of the possible, never the impossible."*

Bradbury wonders why this type of novel is so neglected and he gives an example his *Fahrenheit 451*, a novel I never read but a story I remember vividly in its film version. In talking about the novel he says:

> *Take Fahrenheit 451. You're dealing with book burning, a very serious subject. You've got to be careful you don't start lecturing people. So you put your story a few years into the future and you invent a fireman who has been burning books instead of putting out fires...and you start him on the adventure of discovery.... He reads his first book. He falls in love. And then you send him out into the world to change his life. It's a great suspense story, and locked into it is this great truth you want to tell, without pontificating.*

Bradbury's interview opened my eyes to broader notion of the novel of ideas, one that also includes utopian and dystopian fiction, and to a view of science fiction that I've not taken seriously before. In their own way they are just as much novels of ideas as those Goldstein mentions or, indeed, that she writes.

I've read so few of the standard lists of philosophical novels. They are almost uniformly classics or early 20th century novels. I find the language and structure of most of them very slow going, with truths buried deep below the narrative, in most cases a very lengthy one. In both respects, they are quite unlike their more contemporary forms, a few of which I'll review.

> *But I discovered early that I liked ideas much better than people and that was the end of my loneliness."*
>
> Rebecca Goldstein

Some weeks ago in my search for a novel of intellectual debate with a good story thrown in, as well, I recalled *The Mind Body Problem* by Rebecca Goldstein. I read it many years ago, so long ago, it predated my commonplace book. Goldstein majored in philosophy at college, earned her doctorate in the discipline and subsequently returned to her alma mater to teach several philosophy courses. She wrote *The Mind Body Problem* during a summer vacation break.

> *I had just come through a very emotional time....Suddenly, I was asking the most*

> unprofessional' sorts of questions (I would have snickered at them as a graduate student), such as how does all this philosophy I've studied help me to deal with the brute contingencies of life? How does it relate to life as it's really lived? I wanted to confront such questions in my writing, and I wanted to confront them in a way that would insert `real life' intimately into the intellectual struggle. In short I wanted to write a philosophically motivated novel.

This is exactly what she accomplished in this novel and why I both recalled it, which isn't always the case for one I read a long time ago, to say nothing of those I read last month. The novel begins with a question. At once you know a philosopher is a work here. *"I'm often asked what it's like to be married to a genius."*

Thereafter, Goldstein proceeds to unravel what it was like for Renee Feuer who enrolls as a graduate student in philosophy at Princeton where she meets the legendary mathematical genius, Noam Himmel, that she marries. They squabble, battle over intellectual puzzles, he treats her disdainfully, she has affairs, and along the way delves deeper into the mind-body problem. Renee describes it this way: how is it possible to reconcile the *"outer place of bodies and the inner private one of minds."* Sex versus cerebration as one person aptly put it.

In a recent interview Goldstein was asked, "What is love?" She answers rather elliptically but thoroughly true to life.

What is love? ... we all want good things to happen to ourselves and keep the bad things at bay. You know when you love somebody you want that as much for them if not more than you do for yourself. I mean that is just the world has to go right for them or you won't be able to bear it. ...

The novel ends with an expression of her answer. Within a few years, Noah loses his mathematical prowess. *"I don't have it anymore. I never knew what it was when I had it, and now I don't have it anymore."* Noah breaks down with his confession. He no longer has the power to create or the desire as well and for a mathematical genius you need both.

A few years ago, Goldstein was awarded a MacArthur "genius" award. The Foundation announced:

Rebecca Goldstein is a writer whose novels and short stories dramatize the concerns of philosophy without sacrificing the demands of imaginative storytelling. ... Goldstein's writings emerge as brilliant arguments for the belief that fiction in our time may be the best vehicle for involving readers in questions of morality and existence.

Suppose therefore a person...to have become perfectly well acquainted with colours of all kind, excepting one particular shade of blue...Let all the different shades of that colour, except that single one, be placed before him...Now I ask, whether it is possible for him, from his own imagination,

> *to supply this deficiency, and raise up to himself the idea of that particular shade, though it had never been conveyed to him by his senses.*
>
> David Hume

We are in Edinburgh. Edgar Logan, a young man from Paris, arrives to translate the essays of David Hume. *"...most of my life has been spent in books, reading other people's stories, living vicariously through characters that don't exist."*

Early on he meets the, bitter, physically crumbling, soon-to-be-dismissed-philosophy professor, Harry Sanderson and his enigmatic wife, Carrie. *"Up until then I lacked the talent for friendship. Later I would sometimes wonder what it was about the Sandersons that made the difference, what it was the sucked me in..."*

This is how Jennie Erdal begins her novel, *The Missing Shade of Blue*. It engrossed me from the first page. Several threads are interlaced throughout her tale.

On David Hume: *Hume had not set out with the intention of being an unbeliever. Rather he had followed the arguments for religion and them wanting. He was a man primarily interested in explaining our place in the world so that we might live better lives; and the art of living well, he soon discovered did not sit happily with clinging on to illusions.*

On philosophy: *The unexamined life is much despised. According to Socrates, it is not worth living. But actually, the examined life can get you into all sorts of trouble.*

On painting: *At that point the language to interpret a painting was simply not available to me. Later Carrie would tell me this was an advantage. My eyes were innocent like those of a child, though to me they were simply crude and ignorant.*

On vicarious experience: *Nearly all of my experience of life—the highs and lows, the hopes and disappointments, the chaotic entanglements—everything that matters in fact—all of this has been mediated through the written word. With the result that novels have given me the sense—the illusion perhaps—of a connection with others, with the texture of real lives.*

On marriage: *My close reading of fiction had taught me that nearly all marriages occupied strange territory. But it was more vivid and startling to see it with you own eyes.*

On happiness: *…happiness often reveals itself as counterpoint. It is edged about with things that are opposite to it.* On novels: *…a good novel was like a small miracle…fiction allowed us to live lives of other than our own….And every so often, I said, something emerged from a novel that could only be called truth—there was no other name for it. Which has a paradoxical ring to it, since of course, fiction is made up, full of lies.*

These are but a fraction of the passages I noted in *The Missing Shade of Blue*. Is there a story along with Erdal's philosophical ruminations? Yes, but on my reading, it plays a minor role. There is the tragic deterioration of a once fine philosopher and an emerging relationship between the Edgar, the translator and Carrie, the painter.

A Philosophical Adventure is the subtitle of *The Missing Shade of Blue*. That it is, the kind of book I am forever searching for. To find one is a "small miracle." For a philosopher, it will be a fictional treat. For a translator or painter, it is an endless debate. For any reader, it is a rich dialogue on Hume, happiness, friendship, language, and should you be the least bit interested, fly-fishing.

And philosophy was the pure song, the purest of songs, heard only with training, and hanging at a pitch outside of the common range.

Samantha Harvey

Samantha Harvey invites a reader to consider several issues throughout her philosophical novel, *All is Song*—the power of brotherly love, the choice between questioning and conforming, and the pervasiveness of anti-intellectualism in society.

Not everyone likes this kind of novel. One reviewer found the writing "labored." Another commented on the "overwhelming beauty of the prose." So much for critical reviews.

Leonard Deppling returns to London after the end of his marriage and caring for his dying father. He has come to join his brother, William, a former lecturer and activist. Leonard seeks to understand why William never visited his ailing father or attended his funeral. He moves in with William, his wife and three children.

William is a thoroughly unconventional man, unworldly, and forever questioning. What? How? Why? He is a modern version of Socrates, walking about the neighborhoods of London, talking informally with young people, and gathering quite a dedicated group of followers. He says,

> *...to my mind, far from being arrogant, asking questions is the most humble thing a person can do. And my freedom isn't a reward if it's at the expense of reason and honesty.*

Imagine being with such a person, a person who never ceases to question what you say never assuming he understands what you said, or that you understood it either. He takes the simplest thing you say and breaks it down into little linguistic puzzles. What do you mean by this? The word has several meanings. I am not sure what you meant by this. William says,

> *The problem is that you've used a lot of ideas in that sentence I can't even begin to understand. The just, the good, the natural.*

Leonard gathers himself together and says, "*Allow me a sentence free of charge sometimes; allow me that, yes?* William replies, "*I won't do anything without proper thought.*"

Finally, one of William's young followers, Stephen, commits a crime that for any serious reader is one of the worst imaginable. Stephen flees the country and because of the close association of the two men, William is implicated in the crime.

Recall what happened to Socrates when he was accused of corrupting the youth of Athens. William acts similarly during his trial as an accessory to the crime. He says, *"I'd rather share elbow room in a prison cell than give away a millimeter of space in my mind."*

In spite of William's questioning and the dispute this usually led to, nothing he could say or do had slightest effect on the deep bond between the two brothers. The kindness and love between them remained in tact.

I see kindness at times among all the bullshit, and I see love.

What I see in Nature is a magnificent structure that we can comprehend and only very imperfectly, and that must fill a thinking person with a feeling of humility. Albert Einstein

Zia Haider Rahman's *In the Light of What We Know*, is a magnificent book. Not for the story that meanders about in a disjointed fashion. But for the ideas, the abundance of ideas and the questions that lead only to more ideas and questions.

It is a philosophical tour-de-force and if you like philosophical fiction, *In the Light of What We Know* will delight you, as it did for me on almost every one of its 500 pages.

The story is straightforward: one day a bedraggled man arrives at the south Kensington (London) door of a well-healed investment banker. The nameless narrator soon recognizes Zafar, his great friend at Oxford and later in the New York and London financial world.

Zia Haider Rahman was born in Bangladesh, was raised in poverty, came to England as a boy, where his father was a bus conductor. He gained a place at Oxford, excelled in mathematics, went on to study at Cambridge and Yale and eventually worked in finance, thereafter as an international human rights lawyer.

In these respects, his life mirrors that of the fictional Zarfar. It appears as if the nameless narrator is in fact, the author, with Zafar his fictional counterpart, and the two in an autobiographical dialogue to understand the life of Zia Haider Rahman.

Zafar is invited to stay at the narrator's home as long as he wants and the two friends begin talking, day after day, about their respective lives, mostly Zafars' who eventually left investment banking to become a lawyer and later an NGO representative in Afghanistan.

The narrator's life is in shambles, his childless marriage has all but ended, as has his work as a mortgage-backed securities trader, where his dealings in complex derivatives has been called into question. Yet all the while, he had been encouraged by central bankers, governments and the partners in his firm to take those risks, risks that in the end were enormously profitable to his partners, who he had counted as his friends.

He also realizes that the choices he made failed to express his truest self and he never needed the money anyway, as he had been favored with a family fortune. And so he wonders if in recounting Zafar's life he might learn something about how things could have been better.

I am reminded of a similar question Pascal Mercier poses in writing about the life of the

Portuguese scholar and physician, Amadeu de Prado. In *The Goldsmith of Words*, Prado asks, "*Can we better understand ourselves by studying the life of someone else?*" The question leads Gregorious, the protagonist of the novel, to abandon his post at his school in Basel in a quest to learn as much as he could about Prado, his family, friends and life he led in Lisbon.

In the Light of What We Know also includes a fair amount of Zafar's on and off love affair with Emily Hampton-Wyvern, whose father was an eminent judge and family an entirely different class than Zafar's. The difficult relationship between the classes in England underlies much of Rahman's characterization of Zafar and his thwarted loved affair with Emily.

Ideas abound from the first words, the first chapter and it soon becomes clear that the novel will be a philosophical discussion about the varieties of knowledge and the sources of truth. At the beginning of each chapter, Rahman cites one or more epigraphs. In the first there is one on Exile:

> *Exile is strangely compelling to think about but terrible to experience. It is the unhealable rift forced between a human being and a native place, between the self and its true home: its essential sadness can never be surmounted. And while it is true that literature and history contain heroic, romantic, glorious, even triumphant episodes in an exile's life, these are no more than efforts meant to overcome the crippling sorrow of estrangement. The achievements of exile are permanently undermined by the loss of something left behind forever.*
>
> Edward W. Said, *"Reflections on Exile."*

Zafar never really felt at home in the world he had created for himself, always felt an exile from his roots and all that he had known before coming to Oxford. This was true in his relationship with the privileged, flirtatious Emily Hampton-Wyvern, a woman who he never felt was quite believable or who accepted him, in spite of his admiration of her family and her unpredictable, half-hearted expressions of love. Rahman writes:

> *Zafar was an exile, a refugee, if not from war, then of war, but also an exile from blood. He was driven, I think, to find a home in the world of books, a world peopled with ideas, whose companionship is offered free and clear, and with the promise that questions would never long be without answers or better questions.*

At its core, *In the Light of What We Know* is a discussion of the search for truth and the danger of metaphorical models of understanding. The only certainty is to be found in mathematics where, if the math is correct, there cannot be any doubt about what is proved.

Rahman seems extremely dubious of what we claim to know, believes it is essential to question everything. The narrator's father, a physicist, says to him one day, *"My point is that you could think of the people you meet in your life as questions, there to help you figure out who you are, what you're made of, and what you want. ... It's only when the particles rub against each other that we figure out their properties. ...It's when the thing interacts that its properties are revealed, even resolved."*

Yet at other times Rahman doubts the value of metaphors. While they are tools that give us a sense of something, they can be quite misleading. Truth is far richer and more complex than metaphors imply and while they provide some information, they may lead us down a path that is really no information at all.

He cites Richard Feynman, who in 1965 received the Nobel Prize in Physics. Feynman believe that *"an explanation of something by reducing it and simplifying it over and over, until all that's left is some familiar metaphor that is actually without content, helps no one's understanding of the thing itself and is only the repetition of a familiar image."*

Believing that you know something can also be a source of error. In the case of perceptional illusions, knowing they are illusions doesn't guarantee you will see them correctly. Rahman writes, *"Stare at the image as much as you like, it's all in vain. It will never surrender the truth, not to your naked eyes; you have to go in armed with a straightedge."* The correctness of this view has been confirmed over and over again in the laboratory.

In the Light of What We Know comes face-to-face with the limits of knowledge, memory, perception, knowing our self, and international aid programs. The nameless narrator writes, *"I know he* [Zafar] *knew that mathematics would never answer all or any of the questions of human life and suffering, but the dream was that in her own land, in her own fertile crescent, mathematics would at least yield answers to her own questions and never, instead, mock the traveler with barren wells, never deny him the proof of how those crystalline truths are true at all.*

The novel reminds us over and over that we know less than we think we do, that metaphors are a poor method of reaching the truth, that memories are often distorted and refashioned over time and that doubt and intellectual modesty is the source of wisdom.

Zafar had set himself to the pursuit of knowledge, and it is apparent to me now, in a way it was not before, that he had done so not in order to "better himself," as the expression goes, but in order to lay ground for his feet to stand upon; in order, that is, to go home, somewhere, and take root.

I believe that he had failed in this mission and had come to see, as he himself said in so many words, that understanding is not what this life has given us, that answers can only beget questions, that honesty commands a declaration not of faith but ignorance, and that the only mission available to us, one laid to our charge, if any hand was in it, is to let unfold the questions, to take to the river knowing not if it runs to the sea, and accept our place as servants of life.

Does Literature Change Lives?

I was changed by literature, not by cautionary or exhortatory literature, but by the truth as I found it in literature. I recognize the world in a different way because of it, and I continue to be influenced in that way by it. Opened up, made more alert, and called to a greater truthfulness in my own accounting of things, not just in my writing, in my life as well. It did that for me, and does that for me, and no one touched by it in this way should have any doubt of its necessity.

Tobias Wolff

How are readers influenced by their reading experiences? Do readers of literary works behave differently after their reading experiences than they would have otherwise? Or how are their beliefs or values changed by books they have read? The experience of reading a work of literature is rarely if ever, included among the influential agents of personal change. Yet many people report that it was a book that changed the course of their life or the lives of a large group of individuals. Goethe's *Sorrows of Young Werther* is perhaps the foremost example of the powerful impact of the reading experience. It led so many young individuals into acts of imitative suicide that it was banned in several countries soon after it was published.

Less dramatic effects have recently been reported on several sites on the Web. The San Francisco bookstore, A Clean Well-Lighted Place for Books, has a page on its website that invites readers to "name the book that changed your life." One contributor responded: *"The Harry Potter books changed my life. I used to hate reading. Now I am the best reader in the class. Those books changed my imagination. I wasn't too much of a dreamer. Now, I love to imagine things. I just hope that they change someone else's life like they did mine."*

The Autodidactic Press also offers a similar invitation on the "Books that Changed Lives" page on its website. In citing *The Autobiography of Malcolm X*, one individual wrote: *"I first read the book as a sixth grader. The book was so searing that I vowed to become like that unusual man. Today I am a Muslim as a direct result of Malcolm's autobiography."*

The Academy of Achievement seeks to bring young students in this country into contact with the "greatest thinkers and achievers of the age." To encourage young individuals to develop a love of books the Academy has created a website, that has posted the responses of individuals it regards as "eminent achievers, to the question "What book did you read when you were young that most influenced your life?"

To date the Academy has recognized 142 achievers in five areas: the arts (46), business (14), public service (40), science (30) and sports (12). Its Web site has posted detailed interviews with each of these individuals about their past and the keys to their success. Among the questions asked was one on notable books they had read in their youth: *"What book did you read when you were young that most influenced your life?"* The edited responses from individuals in three of the groups are shown below:

Arts: Joyce Carol Oates

> The one book, probably, of my young adolescence would have been Henry David Thoreau's Walden. That struck a very deep chord with me..... I think that I probably have grown up to have a Thoreauvian perspective on many things. He believed one should simplify, simplify, simplify.

Business: Steve Case

> One in particular that actually was a meaningful impact in terms of what I ended up doing -- focusing on interactive service and the Internet -- was a book I read in college in the late 1970s by Alvin Toffler called The Third Wave....This was 1979, and most people 25 years ago thought I was a little bit loony, but I just believed. And so I just kept pursuing that.

Public Service: President Jimmy Carter

> When people ask me what's a favorite book that I've ever read, I used to say Let Us Now Praise Famous Men by James Agee ... who wrote about the lives of people who lived in desperate poverty.... What impressed me with that book was the tremendous chasm between people who have everything, who have a house and a job and education and adequate diets, and a sense of success or security ...and the vast array of people still in our country who don't have any of these things,....and we are not doing much about it.

The way in which literature can shape a person's life has recently been the subject of three books. In the first, *The Book That Changed My Life*, by Roxanne Coady and John Johannessen 71 authors who gave a reading at the first author's bookstore were asked to write a short passage about a book that had a major effect on their life. In most cases, they wrote about a book that led them to become a writer. After reading the *Bluest Eye* by Toni Morrison, Dorothy Allison wrote: *"If I could repay a tenth of what I owed this storyteller, this brave and wonderful woman on the page, I would give anything."* And Frank Rich, former drama critic of the *New York Times*, wrote: *"Act One [by Moss Hart] showed me a way out of my childhood. If Moss Hart could escape his circumstances through hard work, luck, the kindness of strangers, and the sheer force of his passion, maybe I could too."*

Harriet Scott Chessman described a rarely mentioned book, Gertrude Stein's *Ida*. Chessman comments: *"I loved this striking book for the courage it gave me to start looking for my own "genius," my own spirit, and my own writing life. Stein's influence was slow but profound."* It is clear that many of the books mentioned by the writers have had a life-long influence on their life. Anita Diamant wrote: *"Virginia Woolf's A Room of One's Own influenced me as a journalist and as a novelist in ways that continue to unfold."*

The books selected by these writers constitute a mixture of literary fiction, poetry, drama, biography, history, memoir, and unlikely volumes such as the Sears Catalogue. Several writers mentioned books they had read as children—Nancy Drew Mysteries,

Charlotte's Web, A Child's Garden of Verse, The Little Engine That Could. But literary fiction including both classical and contemporary novels, and in a few instances short story collections were the most commonly identified genre. Taken together as Coady writes in the Introduction to their volume these accounts are *"a dramatic reminder that everywhere, every day, someone is changed, perhaps even saved, by words and stories."*

A somewhat broader sample of individuals was drawn upon in Canfield and Hendricks volume, *You've Got to Read This Book*. The idea for this book emerged during a meeting of "transformation leaders, business consultants, and authors" who had gathered at the home of Jack Canfield to discuss ways to make the "world a better place." During a break, the topic of books came up and several members spoke of the books that had a major influence on their life.

When the group reassembled, Gay Hendricks asked each person to describe a book that had changed their life. Hendricks notes, *"What happened next was wonderful to behold."* Each person spoke with an enthusiasm that "absolutely glowed." This experience led Canfield and Hendricks to conduct in-depth conversations" with 55 people about the books that had this sort of impact on their lives. In turn, the conversations were edited and reorganized by an associate into short essays about the way these books had shaped their life.

It is not entirely clear how the 55 individuals, whose edited accounts are presented in *You've Got to Read This Book!* were selected. They appear to be chosen because they had some acquaintance with the authors and, in one way or another, because they were "all doing valuable work in the world." They were from a variety of fields with the majority in the "self-help movement" including spiritual counselors, personal coaches, and motivational speakers. A large number came from the fields of marketing and technology and several were either writers or publishers.

It is also evident that a goodly number wore many hats, combining work in business and writing and personal training etc. For example, Pat Williams, the senior vice present of the NBA's Orlando Magic is described as a motivational speaker, author of numerous books and marketing guru. He and his wife are also the parents of 19 children, 14 of whom have been adopted from foreign countries. Another contributor, Tim Ferriss, is characterized as *"an accelerated-learning researcher, world traveler, and guest lecturer at Princeton University."* He is also said to be fluent in Japanese, Mandarin Chinese, German and Spanish and holds a title in Chinese kickboxing and a Guinness world record in tango, coached more than 80 "world champion athletics and the author of several books. We should all have such talent.

An overwhelming majority of book-induced effects were changes in a person's beliefs, commitments, or intentions to act. In addition, each such change was usually preceded by a dilemma in the person's life that the book dealt with and offered a solution.

Ten readers described relatively specific changes the book motivated them to undertake including being more sociable or goal directed and, in the case of five individuals, emphasizing the importance of controlling the course of one's life and taking responsibility for one's actions.

> *I pulled it [Psycho-Cybernetics by Maxwell Maltz] off the shelf, started reading, and found it was easy to read and made a lot of sense. It took the book home and read it cover to cover, and then started again at the beginning. One message stood out for me: You are in control of your destiny. Your mind is very powerful; what you think is your reality.* Rudy Ruettiger

Fifteen readers described a wide range of effects including "lightening up," "doing what is right," trusting your instincts or desires, taking risks and being more courageous.

The most frequently noted effects were spiritual/cognitive changes that were noted by 17 contributors. Gaining understanding or insight about an event in their life was the most often mentioned (8), followed closely by those who turned toward a more spiritual life (7) with 2 individuals reporting a book that helped them to "find the real me" or gain a greater sense of their own identity.

> *I had been trying to control things that were fundamental uncontrollable and the cost had been the moment-by-moment disruption of my peace of mind. ...But now with the help of Epictetus [The Book of Life] I realized the pointlessness of trying to control my emotions. They have a life of their own, and they will last as long as they last. Applying the wisdom Epictetus conveys in his first sentence, I relaxed my resistance, letting go of my*

> *effort to wish my feelings away....That brief moment in time exerted such a powerful positive influence on me that it has affected the way I live my life and practice my profession ever since.* Gay Hendricks

In spite of their limited representativeness, these anecdotal accounts leave little doubt that books can be powerful agents of change for a wide range of individuals. It is also abundantly clear that a multiplicity of books can have this effect--from the *Sears Catalogue* to, *Instant Replay: The Green Bay Diary of Jerry Kramer*, *Don Quixote* to Homer's *Odyssey* and Aristotle's *Ethics*. This indicates that whatever influence the experience of reading a book might have, it will be highly personal. In all the accounts I've mentioned rarely was a book cited more than once and those that were number less than ten. The Bible was the one exception, although it's impact is not universal, as it was not cited by any of the 71 writers who contributed to the Coady & Johannessen volume and only one of the 55 individuals interviewed by Canfield and Hendricks.

The wide range in the age an influential book is read is also evident from these accounts. Readers recalled books that they read early in their childhood, adolescence and throughout their adult life. In addition, most indicated they were surprised by the book's impact; it was unexpected, more a matter of happenstance than one intentionally planned. In this respect the experience of reading an influential book is much like the process that occurs when any kind of fortuitous event alters behavior.

Rather than personal testimonials of this sort, I was looking for more general tests of the various hypotheses about the effects of reading literature, tests that would determine how widespread and long lasting such an effect might be compared to the many other ways we attempt to change behavior. I was aware of various theories about the effects of reading literature that date back as far as antiquity, but as far as I could tell, the empirical study of these views under natural reading conditions was virtually non-existent.

It seemed to me then that literary scholars had examined almost everything else about literature except its influence on readers. Robert Wilson put it well: *"Although most persons would agree that reading may be generally efficacious in directing an individual's development, few attempts have been made to define its influence more precisely."* Perhaps the question is simply too complex or too "psychological" for the critics. They may simply assume that reading literature influences individuals, that, indeed, it sometimes affects their thought and personality but that it is hopelessly naive to expect that empirical studies will ever be able to clarify the nature and extent of its influence.

In fairness, writers and critics recognize the importance of the question. In his remarks at the PEN conference, The Power of the Pen, Salman Rushdie acknowledged that while it is unusual for literature to have a major influence on one's life, occasionally readers will fall in love with a book that changes them permanently.

Rushdie referred to Uncle Tom's Cabin that *"changed attitudes toward slavery, and Charles Dickens's portraits of child poverty [that] inspired legal reforms and J.K. Rowling [who] changed to culture of childhood making millions of boys and girls look forward to 800 page novels."* He also noted that occasionally a reader will fall in love with a book that *"leaves its essence inside him...and those books become parts of the way we see our lives; we read our lives through them, and their descriptions of the inner and outer worlds become mixed up with ours—they become ours."* The experience is rare but when it does take place it exerts a powerful and long lasting hold on the reader.

In one of the first in-depth, albeit not experimental, studies I found on the effects of reading literature Martha Purdy analyzed the various forms of learning that occur in reading literary fiction. Purdy conducted comprehensive interviews with five regular novel readers. After coding each interview, she found, not surprisingly, that these readers sought out novels for entertainment and escape. But along the way they also collected new factual information, as well as insights about themselves, their personal beliefs, and values. They did not necessary read with the primary intention of learning, but it was an inevitable consequence of an incidental learning process that characterizes virtually every experience, including that of reading literature.

My search uncovered several investigations of the use of reading experiences as a therapeutic tool. This approach, known as "bibliotherapy," *is the "use of print and non-print material, whether imaginative or informational...to effect changes in emotionally disturbed behavior."* While bibliotherapy was employed initially with individuals institutionalized in prison or mental hospitals, it has recently been extended to other community settings, including schools and libraries. All such programs attempt to use the experience of reading written material to change a person's behavior, attitudes or values in some way.

Is bibliotherapy an effective way to change behavior? The behaviorally oriented approaches, during which individuals are asked to read self-help materials in treating problems such as alcoholism, obesity, and social anxiety, appear to be the most successful. But even in these cases the evidence for their effectiveness is mixed. A recent review indicated that it was most effective in the treatment of depression, mild alcohol abuse and anxiety disorders and less successful for smoking cessation and more severe cases of alcohol abuse. In contrast, reading fiction, poetry, or creative non-fiction as a self-help tool appears to have only a modest degree of influence that is most clearly reflected in attitude rather than behavioral change. However, the research in this area is not extensive and what has been done is methodologically far from elegant.

I have somewhat similar concerns about the studies reported by Hakemulder in *The Moral Laboratory*. Hakemulder summarizes the results of a large number of investigations on the effects of reading narrative passages on attitudes and moral beliefs. Unfortunately, the studies he describes varied widely in their outcomes with few statistically significant results. Moreover they were carried out in the laboratory under highly reactive test conditions in which the individuals were asked to read specially prepared segments rather than intact works of literature. In my view, research with individuals engaged in natural reading experiences seems far more likely to capture the effects of literature than such artificial laboratory situations.

Consider, for example, recent research on some of the newly emerging programs designed to introduce literature to economically and educationally disadvantaged individuals. Most are based on the interdisciplinary humanities curriculum developed by Earl Shorris, known as the Clemente Course in the Humanities. The eight-month course in poetry, logic, art, history, and moral philosophy described in Shorris's book *Riches for the* has been adopted at several locations throughout the country, with a goal of fifty such programs in the coming years. According to Shorris, the intensive study of the humanities is an effective way to move people out of poverty and into community engagement and meaningful work.

How successful is the course in achieving this goal? Gathering evidence to answer this question is not easy. It is often difficult to track down participants in the courses, many of whom lead chaotic lives with no permanent addresses or phone numbers. Shorris reports a preliminary evaluation in the Appendix to his first book, *New American Blues: A Journey through Poverty to Democracy* (Norton, 1996). Only half (55%) of the students were able to complete the course the first time he offered it, leaving a sample of seventeen individuals for the pre- and post-course assessment analysis. The findings indicated there were modest gains in the student's self-esteem and use of cognitive strategies. But most of the change scores were not significant, and absent comparative data from a group of individuals who were not able to participate in the course or were enrolled in an alternative program, it is difficult to know what to make of these findings.

Slightly better evidence is available from a class in humanities offered by faculty at Stanford University to groups of fifteen to twenty female addicts and ex-convicts who have been placed in a residential (Hope House) drug and alcohol treatment program. The Clemente-derived course offered at Hope House focuses on classic texts, with an emphasis on political and social issues. Follow-up evidence from the women who have participated in this program revealed that approximately 70% have remained drug free and out of prison, a value that the authors describe as "far better than the national average."

In the tradition of these studies, the Portland-based Oregon Council of Humanities, in collaboration with nearby Reed College, offers a free, two-semester, college level course in the humanities to low-income individuals with limited education. Recently the course was introduced to a group of incarcerated inmates at medium-security adult male correctional facility in Eastern Oregon. The course, known as Humanity in Perspective (HIP) seeks to provide the knowledge and intellectual skills that can foster significant changes in the lives of the participants. It is based on the conviction that all individuals, no matter what their life histories or economic circumstances, can learn to live better lives once they have the opportunity to explore the great literature and ideas of the past and present.   In the Fall semester students read key Ancient Greek works drawn from texts in history (Thucydides), philosophy (Aristotle & Plato), poetry (Tyrtaeus & Sappho), and drama (Sophocles & Euripides). In the Spring Semester readings are selected from more contemporary texts including Emerson, Thoreau, Mark Twain, Flannery O'Connor, Tennessee Williams, Martin Luther King and Toni Morrison.

I was recently given an opportunity to evaluate the course. A questionnaire was developed in order to compare the student's responses both before and after they participated in the course. The survey consisted of three sections designed to assess the impact of the course in a number of areas including literary activities, critical thinking, writing ability and self-esteem. The results in both settings indicated that the course exerted considerable influence on a wide range of student attitudes and beliefs.

The students in Portland displayed a significant improvement in their level of self-esteem, verbal ability, and in their analysis of the major course themes. It also had a positive impact on the inmates who displayed an overall positive change in their literary activity, writings skills, and their treatment of the major course themes.   These findings should be tempered somewhat by the fact that the samples were small and there was considerable variation between the students and settings in which the course was offered. For instance, the two groups were not evenly matched, especially in terms of educational background. Unlike the students in Portland, most of the inmates had enrolled in GED and other education courses offered at the institution. As a result, they had recent educational experiences that were directly assessed in the survey, whereas many of the students in Portland had been out of school for several years or had never participated in any non-school educational programs.

The inmates were also highly motivated to enroll in the class, while it was difficult to recruit students for the course in Portland. Class attendance at the prison was required and the inmates were always escorted to the classroom by a guard. In contrast, the students in Portland often had to drive or take the bus a considerable distance to reach the classroom and, on occasion, missed the evening class because of travel or personal constraints. These difficulties may account for the differing course graduation rates between the two groups: the rate for the course in Portland, over its five-year history, is 41%, while in its first year, the students at the prison had a 86% graduation rate.

In combination, these differences may explain why the course did not have the same effects in the two settings. That is, gains on one measure by participants in one of the groups were not necessarily associated with comparable gains by the students in the other group. It is evident, however, that the humanities course in Portland and the correctional institution exerted considerable influence on the students. The overwhelming impression one gets from examining these data is that the experience of reading and discussing some of the great works of literature went a long way toward meeting the educational goals of the Humanity in Perspective Program and fostering a number of significant changes in the lives of the students.

These findings were supported by uniformly positive reports by the students in both settings. A student who spoke at the Spring 2006 graduation ceremony in Portland eloquently expressed the student's sentiments:

> "My classmates and I answered an invitation to come and learn. Twice a week for 2 semesters we gathered together to discuss some of history's great minds and ideas. We read and discussed the Greek Philosophers and dramatists...the foundations of Democracy in America...the Transcendentalists and contemporary writers...issues of slavery, prejudice, women's right, civil rights, human rights. We wrote papers and formulated thesis arguments. These things alone would constitute an interesting educational experience. But this is not all we learned. We learned that these were not just texts to be read, but ideas to live by. We learned about the power of words to harm or to help. We learned how to listen, and how and when to speak up. We learned that our ideas and our opinions are important. We learned that each of us can make a difference in our lives, in our community, in the world. We learned these

> *things not only from these texts and from our teachers, but from each other."*

To be sure, empirical study of this issue faces a number of conceptual and methodological limitations. There is a lack of specificity in knowing what aspect of the reading material is responsible for the observed effects. Further, most of the studies do little more than establish a relationship between exposure to these materials and changes in attitudes or behaviors, leaving open the question of whether the experience *per se* caused these effects. Finally, the research to date has been based on fairly weak designs, without, for example, comparison or control groups required to rule out alternative accounts of the findings.

Reading great works of literature is not often considered among the foremost sources of personal change. However, evidence reviewed in this essay makes it clear that the experience of reading a book can exert a powerful influence on human thought and action. This is most likely to occur when individuals face a personal problem, when they are primed and searching for a solution. A great many individuals report it was a book that finally pointed them in the direction of one. Yet these encounters were for most part not planned or deliberately induced by an agent of change. This suggests that both practitioners and investigators of the behavior change process may be neglecting the very considerable influence that reading works of literature can have on individuals.